A BRIEF HISTORY OF THE FLOOD

A BRIEF HISTORY OF THE FLOOD

STORIES BY

Jean Harfenist

ALFRED A. KNOPF

NEW YORK

2002

*Some of the stories in this collection were originally published in slightly different form in the
following:* The Barcelona Review: *"Pixie Dust";* Crazyhorse: *"Salad Girls";* Nimrod:
"The Road out of Acorn Lake" (originally entitled "The Road to the City"); Prism
International: *"Fully Bonded by the State of Minnesota";* Quarterly West:
"Duck Season."

Library of Congress Cataloging-in-Publication Data
Harfenist, Jean.
A brief history of the flood / Jean Harfenist — 1st ed.
p.   cm
ISBN 0-375-41393-6
1. Minnesota—Social life and customs—Fiction.   2. Working class families—Fiction.
3. Rural families—Fiction.   4. Young women—Fiction.   5. Girls—Fiction.   I. Title.
PS3608.A73B75 2002
813'.6—dc21   2002019068

For my husband, Stan,
and for my mother, Margaret Olsen Lippka

CONTENTS

1959

Floating

Mom says, "Now this is how it's supposed to be." She smiles her sparkly smile and looks around the breakfast table at all of us while the breeze off the lake comes through the screens and the red squirrels chitter in the oak trees. Our living and dining room are one big square with golden knotty-pine paneling and a high-beamed ceiling. Dad built it that way. Then he nailed deer heads and rifle racks to the walls and named it Jack's Hunting Lodge. But Mom put a sign out by the road with just our name next to a mallard hen: ANDERSON.

Randy always sits next to me. I kick his bare foot and nod at Dad who's jabbing his sliced bananas with his fork, *click-click, click-click* against the Melmac bowl. Randy raises his sun-bleached eyebrows at me, which means just let it go, but Mitzy jumps to her feet, points her skinny finger in Dad's face and says, "Mom says it sets her teeth on edge when you do that." I'll be eight this month, Mitzy's nearly ten and Randy's twelve. Mom looks at Dad. She's biting the tip of her tongue with her tiny white teeth. Dad pokes his bananas faster, like some mad guy knocking on our door, so she goes back to peeling her orange in one long strip using just her thumbnail. Without looking up, she laughs once, and says real loud, "Sure do love all of you."

Randy says, "Love you, Mom."

Mitzy says, "Love you."

I say, "Love you."

Dad rattles his coffee cup on the saucer for a refill, not saying a word even though we're all looking at him. When his upper lip flattens out, we stop looking. Then Mom stands up so fast her chair falls over backward. Her head's turning this way and that, when our black Lab, Happy, howls from the end of the dock with a sound that lifts the rest of us out of our chairs and sets us on our feet. Randy runs fastest, down the lawn. By the time I reach the end of the dock I have to squeeze between Mom and Dad and shove Mitzy aside to see Randy standing waist-high in the lake, holding Davey facedown over his shoulder like a sack of flour, pounding his back while Davey screams like he's being born again, but this time he's nearly two. Randy looks up at Mom and Dad, all huge eyes and big ears, wondering what he's supposed to do now.

When Davey gives a watery gasp it's as if Mom, Dad and Mitzy wake up and jump into the water. Davey's so slippery wet they almost drop him trying to flip him right side up. Then Mom has him tight against her chest. "My baby, my baby." Like My Baby is his real name. She's rubbing her cheek against his even though he threw up and now it's on both of them. Dad says, "For Chrissake, Marion," as if she's done something else wrong. "The kid'll be fine," he says. She looks at him like she can't remember who he is.

Davey is screaming again, shaking his little fists, when I realize I'm the only human being still standing on the dock with the dog. I jump in, hoping no one noticed. I can't stand babies, but I'm picking weeds off Davey now, shivering, just glad he's alive.

Later that morning the four of us kids and Happy are sitting on the floor of our pontoon boat, passing around a saucepan of chicken noodle soup Randy heated. The boat's a big red floating version of Davey's playpen—just a flat wooden deck with side railings, a steering column in the middle, and a little motor on the back. The whole thing sits on two giant aluminum floats called pontoons. We keep it tied to our dock. I let Happy lick soup from my hand, laughing when her tongue tickles my palm. She's a hero.

Davey stands up slowly, looking confused and kind of green from almost drowning. When the wake from a big inboard hits, his arms shoot up like he's surrendering, Randy snags him, hauls him onto his lap, and rearranges his fat baby legs to make him comfortable while we ride it out together, up and down, waiting for Mom.

Mom always says she wanted twelve kids, an even dozen to love her forever, but Dad put his foot down after I was born and it took her six years to sneak in Davey. She likes talking about the eight kids she never had as if they're off waiting somewhere—maybe in the toolshed back by the road. She points to her stomach and says her tubes are tied in knots so we're all she's ever going to have: Randy, Mitzy, me and Davey. And Happy.

Mitzy's sitting with her feet straight out, slapping the backs of her knees against the deck, drinking soup from the pan. She stops and says, "It was your fault, Lillian. You were supposed to watch the baby."

"No I wasn't," I lie. "Randy was."

"You're jealous because you're not the baby anymore."

I eyeball her. I always thought when I watched the baby, Mom was watching both of us, that it was a helping-out job like breaking eggs into the bowl when she bakes brownies.

Mitzy slaps my arm with the spoon, leaving a warm wet speck of noodle. I grab the spoon, fling it over her head into the lake. She shouts, "Goddamnit!" and kicks out at me like a thresher. "Mom's been sleeping too goddamned long."

As if it's up to me. I roll into a ball and cover my head. My sister's thin as a toothpick, but being mean makes her strong.

Randy says, "You don't have to swear, Mitzy."

"But moms shouldn't sleep so long," she says, covering us with spit the way she does every time she says something with an *s* in it, like her tongue's too thick or her lips are too big or her front teeth are too short. Something's wrong with her. She grabs the pan by its handle and sails it out over the lake, where it lands upright, does a couple of slow spins and sinks like the weeds pulled it under. "I'm waking her up."

Ten minutes later Mitzy walks back down the lawn toward us, eating from a tub of chocolate chip ice cream with a new and bigger spoon. Her short hair is already white-blond from the sun, just like Randy's and Davey's. In the winter their hair turns yellow. I'm the only redhead. Mitzy says, "Mom's got the bedroom door locked." She jumps onto the boat, folds herself down onto the deck without missing a bite. "I knocked, but she wouldn't even answer."

Randy asks, "Dad?"

"Must have gone into town."

. . .

6

By one o'clock we've stashed Davey in his playpen on the beach and we're bobbing around in inner tubes. I'm hanging by my armpits, kicking slow, licking the hot black rubber so I can watch the sun dry off the wet mark, when music explodes from the house. Two seconds later Mom's on the patio, dancing by herself in her yellow bikini, elbows in the air, fingers snapping. She was the Minnewashka High School Posture Queen. When Dad's in a good mood, he pats her fanny, tells her she's a looker and they kiss because they're in love.

We paddle toward her as fast as we can.

"See, Mitzy?" I say, kicking my tube onto the grass. "She just needed a nap."

"Shut up."

Mom leaps onto the pontoon boat, light as Tinkerbell, and swivels to face the three of us on the dock. She's perfect except for a scar like a crooked seam where her belly button was before she had Davey, and Dad made her get her tubes tied because she was already in the hospital. Her scar never tans.

"Kids, your mother has an idea," she says. "Mitzy? Drag that roll of chicken wire down here from the ditch across the road, and get all the white paint you can find. Chop-chop. Lillian? Sweetheart? Art supplies. Dry markers, glue. And my sewing kit. Randy, honey, get a bottle for Davey."

We ask what we're going to make, but she just points in the direction she wants us to go and we run off still wearing our wet swimsuits. All summer we get to hang them on the clothesline at night and put them right back on in the morning. We even wear them into town and run squealing through the freezer section of Gill's Grocery.

Later we're on the dock, painting, hammering and tying this to that, music so loud it's like the house is bending its knees, dancing to Louis Prima. Mom says, "Can't you feel that bass in your chest?" holding her breast like her heart's in there. Mitzy grabs herself with both hands where her breasts would be if she had any, turns to Randy, arches her back and slides her hands down her sides and over her hips. He gives her a fake smile, showing every tooth. I say, "Gross."

We sprint to the shed and the woodpile, finding things, then jump into the lake because it's eighty-five degrees and we're sweating like pigs. Having a blast. We race across the sizzling sand—Mom says it only burns if you think about it. She holds up a finger that means *stop!* We wiggle our fingers in the air and shake our bottoms while we sing the chorus: *"So Chattanooga Choo-choo, won't you choo-choo me home? Whoooo-whoooo."* That's the Andrews Sisters.

Mom says, "Drag two stools out onto the boat." We ask, "What's it going to be?" She shouts, "Screwdriver," holding her hand in the air for it. "Mommmmmm." We eat an entire package of Oreos. Mom shouts, "All the snow goose decoys!" Pepsi-Cola, Frosted Flakes. "You kids won't know what I'm creating until it's done." We feed ripple chips to the dog, cookie crumbs to the sunfish that live in the shadow of the dock.

I'm wrapping railings in white crepe paper, Randy and Mitzy are cutting cardboard hearts, when Dad appears on the lawn in his baggy black swim trunks, carrying a tall glass of tomato juice. We're hoping he's out of his mood. Otherwise he'll sit in a lawn chair all day shouting, "Marion, why can't you sit here with your husband for a while?" If Mom's awake, she's working on something.

Dad walks hard on the wooden dock, barefoot, heel-toe, *thud-thud,* pigeon-toed like Mitzy, and thin all over except for a potbelly like a bowling ball. He has a scar across his middle too, a

8

giant frown where the doctors cut out seven-eighths of his stomach because we gave him ulcers. He still pushes there with the heel of his hand when we upset him, and Mom whispers, "Must have been the wrong seven-eighths."

She's standing in the shallow water behind the boat, a paintbrush in her hand, her face paint-speckled white. She's beautiful.

Dad steps to the edge of the dock to look, and his mouth falls open like she's running naked down Main Street. "What in creation?"

She dabs at the motor, lifts her chin. "Tah-dahhhh!!! Tomorrow we're going to win the Fourth of July float contest!"

Randy whistles like a train and we all clap except Dad who points his finger at her like otherwise she couldn't figure out who he's talking to. "For Chrissake, Marion. You don't paint motors."

Randy and I move toward her, but she tilts a hip, cocks her head and winks at Dad. "Darling, later I'll paint your motor any color you want."

After a long drink of tomato juice he smacks his lips. I hate lip-smacking. "After dinner?"

With the tiny tip of her paintbrush, Mom circles the top of the motor again while he watches.

"Heh," he says finally, smiling now, shaking his head because he can't get over how cute she is.

Randy shouts, "Camouflage. Mom, you could paint it camouflage for duck hunting. Gray and green and brown. All swirled together. I could show you."

Dad walks back toward the house.

Mitzy's finger shoots out toward Randy. "Drop dead. It's not a duck-hunting float. Don't be stupid."

Me? I'm hoping for yellow. Mom's favorite color and mine. We paint everything yellow.

We're moving like the wind. We work straight through until dark, when Mom strings extension cords all the way from the house to clamp a spotlight on a dock pole. We can't stop for dinner, but Mom slows down long enough to lift her arms to the sky and twirl, saying in a voice like she's praying, "Star light, star bright," while tiny waves kiss the pontoon floats and the crickets are the loudest you've ever heard.

Later, Randy whispers, "Hey," and points at Dad standing under the front door light. When we look, he shakes his head and goes inside, which is just as well because he would have told Mom not to get carried away when she's just having an up day. When a pointy-winged bat flies fast and low over our heads, we hit the deck, then lie there laughing at ourselves. By ten o'clock we're battling mosquitoes so big that Randy wraps Davey in a towel and runs for the house. Mosquitoes never bite Mom. Her blood's too sweet. Mitzy and I run screaming after Randy, swatting at ourselves. Mom shouts, "Love you." We holler back, "Love you, love you, love you." And it's true.

Early the next morning I rip off my nightgown and pull on the swimsuit I dropped on the floor next to my bed last night. It's cold and wet and there's sand in the crotch. Mitzy's on the other half of our naked bed, sleeping on her knees with her butt in the air, face in the pillow. She only lies down flat when she's going to wet the bed. Right now every mattress in the house is bare because the sheets are on the float.

Downstairs Mom's sleeping on the davenport with one of Dad's undershirts over her bikini, catnapping like she does in the middle of every project. Nothing to worry about. I move her cup of coffee and sit on the floor. Her hands are tucked under the side of her face, squishing her cheek up against her nose. When I touch a blond curl on top of her head, it wraps around my finger, her eyes pop open and she sits up, perky like she's never been asleep in her entire life.

She asks, "You didn't see it yet, did you?"

I shake my head *no.*

"Close your eyes." She takes my hand and leads me outside. The screen door slams behind us as she kneels next to me on the brick patio she laid last summer. She folds an arm around my shoulders, and I rub my nose on her neck for the warm smell of coffee and cigarettes. "Okay, Lily Nilly," she says. "Now open your eyes." She's pointing toward the lake. "Lily, sometimes you need to squint at something before you can tell what it is."

But I can see it perfectly. A wedding cake is floating next to our sagging dock. The bottom layer is a rectangle, and above that are two round layers, a little one on top of a big one. While we watch, the frosting turns from white to buttercream as the sun rises over the hill in the field behind the house.

"When you kids stand on the deck, it'll look like you're standing on the first layer of the cake—like my ring bearers and flower girls. And your dad and I will be the bride and groom on the top layer. And just when we go past the judges? We'll kiss." She kisses my cheek. A big wet kiss.

I can see it all perfectly.

At eleven a.m. our wedding cake is on the move. Randy, Mitzy, Davey and I are lined up on the bottom layer behind the white crepe-papered railing, wearing foil-covered cardboard crowns, and white shirts over our swimsuits. I'm trying not to scratch the green glitter off my face because we're supposed to move our heads around and sparkle when the judge hands us the prize, but the baby oil Mom used to make it stick is itching like chiggers in this heat. It's a cooker of a day; the sun's bouncing off the water so bright we've squeezed our eyes down into little slits.

Up behind us, Mom and Dad are standing on the top layer, wobbling a little because the truth is they're standing on bar stools hidden inside a double-decker chicken-wire silo draped with all our white sheets. Mom rigged yardsticks with baling wire so Dad can drive from up there. She said if he keeps his hands down, no one will be able to tell if anyone is steering. "Like a magic floating wedding cake." She must have used magic to get him onto this boat, because there he is, smiling big, wearing a black top hat left from New Year's Eve and a long-sleeved black shirt over his swim trunks. From the judging stand he'll only show from the waist up, and it'll just look like someone shoved the plastic groom too far down into the wedding cake.

With a jerk on the yardsticks, he aims us toward the boats cutting through the waves, heading for Lazy Acres Beach and Campground—duck boats, ski boats, sailboats, pontoons—coming from everywhere; you've never seen so many boats. Dad's singing loud, *"There'll be bluebirds over the white cliffs of Dover, tomorrow . . ."*

We're quite a sight.

Mom is standing next to him in her white halter-top sundress, Revlon Talk-of-the-Town red lipstick and a pearl necklace I made from Poppit beads. The weight of the floor-length train she sewed to her tiara pulls her head back, lifting her nose in the air. She's holding her aluminum foil magic wand high. I start to tell her brides don't carry magic wands, but Randy elbows me.

Next to me, Mitzy's hanging way out over the railing, waving like the whole world cares that she's on this boat. She turns and shouts through the wind at me, "Isn't this the most fun ever?" foaming at the mouth, turning all those *esses* into *iths*. People say she looks like Dad. Uncle Sven always says it looks like I got off the bus at the wrong house. But I'm like Mom. People don't notice because I have red hair and freckles. I have her bright-green eyes though, and that's what matters. I'm just like her.

Mom and Dad are singing together. You have to strain to hear them over the motors hacking through the water, but they're looking into each other's eyes, singing their song: *"You made me love you. I didn't want to do it . . ."*

Randy and I each have one of Davey's hands. He's waggling his fat body, trying to pull away so he can reach Happy who's howling on the back of the boat.

At the last minute Mom stood on our dock, looking around. "Something's missing. Jack? Don't you feel like something's missing? Jack?"

"Get on the boat, Marion."

Happy whined and Mom called that all-black dog onto her all white wedding cake. She said dogs live for boat rides, so it's hard to tell them no.

Randy scoops up Davey, and I look up just as Dad jerks the yardsticks and we lurch forward in a cloud of gas and motor oil that smells like summer. Mom laughs and whacks him in the chest with her magic wand. He wraps an arm around her, and she leans in to practice their big kiss just as we reach the middle of the bay, where the chop from all the boats comes together, waves smacking each other, shooting water in the air. We're hit from all sides at once—rocked, shaken, jiggled, bounced around like a family of fleas jumping on a bed. Dad lets go of Mom. I shout at Randy, "That baby will sink like a rock if you drop him in. He'll just sink right to the bottom." I can picture it. But we don't even have to hold the railing. We loosen our knees and ride it out like boat ballerinas. We're lake kids.

We reach a calmer spot and pull in behind the Ingebrets' pontoon boat. Dozens of balloons are tied to their railings by long strings. That's it—just balloons. Mr. Ingebret squeezes a bicycle horn at us: *Ah-woooo-gah. Ah-woooo-gah.*

Mom shouts, "What's their theme?"

"Fun," Dad shouts. "It's simple. They're having fun." After a long drink from his metal flask, he starts singing into the wind, and his words drift down on our heads. *"Up a lazy river by the old . . ."*

"But I thought you needed a theme. It has to be about something."

Dad stops singing. "You think too damned much." We swerve out of line because he's steering with one hand and drinking out of his flask with the other.

As the parade curves toward the judging stand, you can see four floats behind ours. The first one's full of clowns. The next two are pirate ships with skull-and-crossbones flags and summer people from the Twin Cities wearing eye patches and waving bottles of booze. Dad shouts, "Yum! Rum!" and toasts them with his flask. But Mom's staring at the last float that pulled into line: It's a farm. A perfect little farm. The Patschkys have three hay bales, a cow, a speckled pig and a wire crate of chickens on their boat. They're wearing checked shirts and straw hats. Mr. Patschky has a pitchfork in one hand. The other hand is on Mrs.

Patschky's shoulder as if they're glued to each other while she kneels milking the cow. The girls—Lana, Ava and Irene—are wearing life belts. It's a known fact farm kids can't swim. Irene is the tallest girl in my grade, and she's always making you pronounce her name: I-*reeeeen* Mar-*leeeeen*-uh *Patch*-key.

Mom says, "But that's not a theme. They're farmers! That's how they live!"

The other eight Patschky girls wouldn't fit on that boat. Dad says farmers don't like kids any better than anyone else but they need them for field hands. My dad's a hardware salesman.

The explosion is a big surprise. I find myself squatting on the deck with my arms covering my head, peeking up to see where it came from. Mom is gone. Dad's blond hair is shining yellow in the sunlight, and smoke is swirling out behind him. He turns toward us, his eyes bluer than the lake. Grinning, he reaches inside his shirt, pulls out another cherry bomb, lights it with his Zippo and lobs it. As it arcs over our heads, Mom rises up from inside the cake, and *blam!* She disappears again.

Mitzy's standing next to me, shaking both fists. She never even ducked. "Goddamnit, Dad! Stop it, just stop it right now!" She stomps her foot, and her crown falls into the water. "You're ruining everything." I stand up, afraid I'm going to cry. Randy shouts, "Dad, why'd you have to do that?" Davey's crying even though he can't see a thing because Randy's still covering his face.

Dad yells, "It's the Fourth of July. And we're Americans."

Mom pops back up.

He shouts, "You're supposed to celebrate." *Blam!*

When she disappears again, her magic wand bumps down the side of the cake and lands at my feet. As I pick it up, I realize we're in front of the judging stand. I lean out over the railing. I smile my biggest smile. I wag my head so my face sparkles, and I wave the magic wand so the judges won't notice the bride is missing from the cake.

The Patschkys win twenty dollars and a lifetime family pass to Lazy Acres Beach and Campground. Maybe they'll teach their kids to swim. People who have to rent a pontoon boat shouldn't be allowed in the parade.

We stand in a clump on the beach, watching people pack up their picnic stuff and wander off. Davey's sitting on my feet, eating sand. I should stop him. Bung Gunderson, owner of Lazy Acres, says hi, pauses, does a U-turn and heads back toward the judging stand, dragging his bad leg in the sand. He sighs into the microphone. "And to the Anderson family goes a special prize." He looks around like some idea is going to jump up and bite him in the ass. "A very special prize." He pulls a six-pack of beer from the ice chest. "The prize for MOST APPROPRIATE goes to the Andersons. Let's all give them a big hand." Nobody does.

Mom runs up onto the grandstand, curtsies and runs back down, smiling, waving the six-pack, but she's faking it. She can't ever fool me.

On the way home, Mom sits on the bottom layer of the cake with us kids, staring at the water. We don't have the energy to shout over the growling motor. As we tie up at our dock, Randy takes her elbow to help her off the boat. "Madam?" he says, like she's a queen.

She says, "Appropriate? Most appropriate?"

Dad's sticking out the top of the cake, leaning forward with his elbows where the frosting is supposed to be. "Don't start."

"What does that mean?"

"Marion—" He takes off his top hat and wipes his forehead with his black sleeve. The two-sided masking tape she used to hold his hat on is stuck to him like a halo.

She plops down on the dock and drops her head between her knees, her full white skirt flounced out, covering every part of her except for one tan leg and a bare foot. Her toenails are the same red as her lipstick. Randy, Mitzy and I stand around her in a circle, Randy holding Davey, bouncing at the knees. I touch Mom's hair with the magic wand. "Mrs. Patschky's fat," I say.

"Marion." Dad jumps off the boat onto the dock with his face clenched tight as a fist. "Why can't you just have a good time like everyone else in the world?"

She doesn't move.

We step back to let him in, hoping he knows how to fix her. He gets behind her, sticks his fingers into her armpits and lifts her a few inches, but she slips back down, so sad she's limp. "Oh, for Chrissake!" he says, looking like he wants to kick her. He turns and stares down into the shallow water next to the dock where the big wooden bait box broke loose and sank to the bottom still full of minnows. He doesn't even look back at her. He just says real slowly, "Why the hell do you always have to make such a big deal out of everything?"

And from between her knees, inside the folds of her skirt, I hear her say, "And why do you always have to make everything smaller than it is?"

For three days since the parade Mom's been resting in the boys' room with Davey, opening the door only twice to stick her hand out for baby bottles, clean diapers and Marlboros. Randy, Mitzy and I have been watching TV, playing poker, fighting, screaming. It won't stop raining.

I'm lying on my back on the rug, checking the ceiling for leaks, when the side door slams. Probably Dad heading for the VFW to brag about his float.

Mitzy says, "Mom should get up." And wooden blocks start raining down on me.

I roll onto my stomach. "She needs her rest." Mom always says the ironing alone is enough to drive a lesser woman to drink. Then she opens her eyes and mouth real wide and shakes her fists and her head like she's screaming. But nothing comes out.

At three o'clock the rain stops, and we wander outside. It's too wet to sit on the picnic table, so we flip the rowboat right side up and push it into the muddy water. Mitzy grabs the narrow seat in the bow. I take the backseat facing Randy.

"Look at my biceps," he says, pulling on the oars so the muscles ride up under his skin like little animals.

"Gross."

Mitzy lisps, "Mom's been sleeping too damned long." She lifts herself off the seat and reaches back to pull her swimsuit out of her crack. She has a big bottom for a skinny girl, and her suit is always going where it's not supposed to.

"Resting," I say. "Mom's just resting."

We stop in the middle of the bay and float around while the waves slap the boat. Randy puts one foot on top of each of mine, and we laugh because his feet are the size of snowshoes. I pull my feet out and put them on his knobby knees. Water dribbles down his calves.

"What if she sleeps forever?" Mitzy says. She starts to rock the boat, leaning side to side. "That could happen."

"She won't," I say.

Mitzy rocks harder, keeping time with her swearing. "Damn it! Sleeping! Damn it! Sleeping!"

"Mitzy," Randy says.

I look at the house. "Mom needs her beauty sleep." I think I see sun glint as if someone opened one of the kitchen windows. You push them out from the bottom, then prop them with a stick. I might have seen one open just now. "Mom's up!"

I wave at the window even though we're too far away to see anything but its outline. Mitzy and Randy wave. We start waving with both hands, yelling, "Mom! Mom! We're out here! Out here! Out here! Out here! Out here!" We're wild, trying to outshout each other, when Randy stands up in the boat, hooks his baby fingers in the corners of his mouth and whistles, one long shriek of a whistle.

After a minute he sits down.

We're quiet again.

"She knows we're here," I say.

"No way," Mitzy says.

"You can't expect Mom to know everything," Randy says, explaining like he always does because he thinks I don't get it. "Not with four kids and a husband and a dog and the cats and three pet rabbits and a house to take care of." He shakes his head. "The ironing alone . . ."

"But she always knows where we are," I say.

"She just says that," Mitzy says, "so you don't go where you're not supposed to."

"Mom knows where we are. And you're stupid."

"Lily Nilly, Lily Nilly. Mom is never coming out of that room again."

"Yeah, because she's sick of looking at you."

"Stop it," Randy says, "or I'll tip the boat over." He leans sideways and pushes one edge close to the water, raising the other side into the air.

"You wouldn't," I say.

"He might," says Mitzy. "He might."

He lets a little water wash over the edge.

"Dad will kill you if you sink this boat."

"It won't sink," he says and lets more water in.

Mitzy turns and stands on the bow seat with her arms out like an airplane, wiggles her bottom at us, then steps up on the point and cannonballs into the water. It's no big deal because we can swim better than we walk, but she doesn't come up right away, so Randy and I are looking around for her when she pops up under our noses, grabs the side of the boat with both hands, lifts herself straight up and pushes down until water rushes in. Randy screams, "TITANIC, TITANIC," leaning out to help her tip the boat. The wooden oar on the high side jumps its lock, and while it bangs down the boat I toss myself off the back and take a stinging nose full of water because I'm screaming, "TITANIC, TITANIC."

I come up and find the boat floating upside down with no sign of Mitzy or Randy, so I dive down to look around, swimming through the weedy water with my eyes wide open, something neither of them can do. Their bodies are hanging down in the water, two sets of legs moving like eggbeaters. I surface next to them under the boat where we can breathe together from a big pocket of trapped air.

"Stay in here!" Mitzy says. "Let's scare Mom."

"I thought you said she doesn't know where we are." Sounds like we're inside someone's head cold.

"She'll figure it out," Randy says.

We wait, treading water in the near dark. The waves ripple against the aluminum boat with an echoey *glug, glug, glug-glug, glug*—missing a beat like a heart murmur. Mom always lets us lie next to her and put an ear on her chest to hear her heart skip. She got her heart murmur from hard times when she was little.

Now Randy sprays water between his front teeth at Mitzy and me. We do it back. The air in here smells like dead carp. I hold my breath and let my body float to the surface, waiting for something to happen. "What will she do?"

"She'll be so scared," Mitzy says, looking pleased. "She'll swim right out here."

"No way," Randy says. "She'll rescue us with the pontoon boat." It's still tied to the dock. The first raindrops melted our names off the cardboard hearts, and then the sheets got so heavy with water that the third layer of the cake caved into the second, and the second collapsed onto the deck. All the chicken wire is showing, looking like chicken wire now.

I'm freezing. "Mom knows we're safe."

"Listen," Mitzy says. She takes a deep breath. "HELLLLLP," she screams as loud as she can, her voice bouncing around in the wet, closed air. Randy screams louder. "HELLLLLP!" I join him, and pretty soon we're just three fishing bobbers under a boat but we're screaming and screaming. Trying it out.

Then we're bored again. It doesn't seem like anything is going to happen, so we dive down and swim out from under the boat to look around. You can't see our house when you're down this low in the water. Randy shows Mitzy and me how to flip the boat back over so it has barely any water in it. You have to balance it perfectly, then push up and flip it fast. Lightweight boats flip easy as long as you don't let them get suctioned to the surface.

Randy climbs into the boat and pulls us in. One of the oars floated off, so he sits on the narrow seat in the bow, paddling Indian style, on one side, then the other. Even if you lose both your oars, you can still get to shore. You have to stay in the water, hang on to the back of a boat and start kicking. You just keep kicking, kicking, kicking. And even if the worst thing happens? If your entire boat sinks? You can still make it. You just need to know how to rest every so often by floating on your back. Taking deep breaths will raise your body to the surface like a balloon. But you can't afford to think about anything else, like how far it is to shore, or how long it'll take to swim it or whether you'll be punished for letting the boat sink. Mostly you better not think about drowning. You have to let it all go and float along until you've got the strength to swim. Otherwise you're a goner.

Mom knows that. And she taught it to us when we were little because she knows we're all she's ever going to have. Randy, Mitzy, me and Davey.

1965

Body Count

*R*andy is going to shoot himself in the foot. He's sitting on the edge of his unmade bed in his underwear with the tip of his shotgun pressed up tight against the big toe of his right foot, his best friend, Tuna, standing next to him, looking down with his head cocked like he's working out some tricky algebra problem. Randy pulls the trigger, screams "Pow!" and jerks his body backward like it's the kick of the twelve-gauge. As he ricochets forward, his yellow hair flops into his eyes. Two seconds later he falls back and lets the shotgun slide to the floor. "Man," he says, "we'll never do it."

I'm sitting on the other bed. They're eighteen and I'm only fourteen, but they like me so much it's as if I'm not even here, so I get to listen to everything. I like knowing what they do with girls.

"Sure we will," Tuna says, grinning. He's the only bald boy in Acorn Lake. "We can do it." He could be right, because Randy'll do anything. He's always first to cross the creek after it freezes, walking on ice so thin it bulges up in front of his boots. And if things get too serious around here, he'll run barefoot through snowdrifts, lapping the front window until we're cracking up. Even Dad. Randy'll do anything.

I'm nibbling on a strand of hair, picturing Tuna daring Randy to shoot himself in the foot tonight while I'm baby-sitting at the Coach's house. Like when they were six and Tuna dared him to run through a sticker bush—eyes open. Randy's eyes look like pennies, and there's a penny-colored fleck in the white part where the doctor pulled the sticker out. Mom called him her brave little soldier, and later for a whole summer Randy, Mitzy and I played brave soldier in the cornfield. I'd like to play it again, maybe once, but if I told them, they'd laugh.

"Randy," I say, "it'd be a waste to shoot yourself before you get your draft notice."

An hour later I'm in the living room. I'm a girl with a plan. "Mom, do you know where Randy and Tuna went?"

The Christmas tree smell is so strong it feels like I'm drinking it. Every year Mom swears she can eyeball a tree on a lot and tell its height within half an inch, then brings one home that's ten inches too tall and has to saw off the base. And Dad gets pissed off because he doesn't want to help, but he doesn't want us watching him not help either.

"Mom?" She doesn't hear me because she's in her perky Christmas mood, trying to make up for Dad who's sitting in his fake-leather armchair, his arms resting on the chair arms, his feet flat on the floor, his eyes staring straight ahead. He looks like a man strapped to an electric chair—a man drinking his last Grain-belt beer strapped to an electric chair that's parked in the middle of our living room, forcing us to walk around him so we don't block his TV. We call this his fair-to-middlin' mood.

I wander around dropping hints like boulders, waiting for someone to get it. "Did Tuna get his draft notice yet?" And like it's an answer, Mitzy says, "You're stupid to sit for Coach Christian." She's sixteen, but she still lisps when she's mad. Her blond hair's cut short as a swimming cap. Mom says we were fighting before I was conceived. Mitzy says, "You don't want to sit for the Coach." But she should have thought of that before she said no when he called to ask her. Everyone says he's the best payer in Acorn Lake, which is exactly why she screamed, *You can't baby-sit there!* when I volunteered. *Toooo late,* I said. *Too late, Mitzy.*

She's standing by the naked tree holding the wooden Virgin Mary her Catholic boyfriend gave her last year. He was making the whole manger scene for her in shop class last spring, but she dumped him for someone else when she only had the Virgin and four of the sheep. Three weeks later I was under the floating dock at Lazy Acres Beach with him and we were kissing like crazy. She went wild when I told her. Too late, Mitzy.

I ask real loud, "Did Randy and Tuna take the shotgun?"

Davey's kneeling on Mom's Early American rug, sorting ornaments on the davenport. He's eight and skinny, but his cheeks are lumpy baby fat. Without looking up, he shakes his head no.

"Shotgun shells? Did they take a box of shells?"

Mom's holding the plastic mistletoe in the air. She's wearing her green felt elf's cap with the jingle bells, her red sweater and her tight kelly-green pants. She winks at me and tiptoes toward Dad, moving like some sneaky cartoon character, then leaps into his lap and kisses his face all over, wild as the dog first thing in the morning. Dad pulls his head this way and that, holding his beer bottle out to one side. "Jesus Christ, Marion! You're spilling my damned beer here." She might as well push a sharp stick through a chain-link fence at a mean dog, because he could explode. Sometimes when he's fair-to-middlin' she does that. I asked her why once, and she said she had never done that. Now she wraps her arms around his neck, wiggles her bottom, leans back, crosses her legs and points her toes, and he says more softly, "Jesus, Marion." Then he sits there with tight little pissed-off lines running down from the corners of his mouth while she looks around at Mitzy, me and Davey, smiling. "Your mother just *loves* love," she says.

Dad slips both hands under her and lifts her off his lap like throwing a sandbag in a flood. He's trying to watch the five o'clock news, waiting for the day's body count from Vietnam so he can say, *My boy.* Five minutes later his eyes get teary. "My boy," he says and puts his hand in front of his eyes as if Randy's hiding in a jungle hut instead of out on the frozen lake, whipping louies in *Sardine II.* That's Tuna's latest junker. When you hit the brakes out on that ice, it feels like you'll spin forever. I know that's where they are. I'm the only one who pays attention around here.

"Dad," I say.

His eyes are dry again. He doesn't look at me, so I walk over to him, careful not to block the TV. "A teacher in school said a boy in Wisconsin shot himself in the foot so he wouldn't get drafted."

"Coward," he says. "Moron."

"It could happen, couldn't it?"

He always says I ask more questions than any damned girl he ever heard of. Now he says, "Every last hippie should land on

Omaha Beach just once in their life. Taste a real man's war." His ship never got to the real war, but it could have.

"Someone might do it though," I say. "On a dare?"

He's watching the war on TV.

I'm getting antsy. I have to go baby-sitting. I'm short on time. "So. Which do you think would be better? To shoot your own foot?" I point at my loafer. "Or let some Vietcong shoot you in the chest?" I step between Dad and the TV and point at my heart, but he leans sideways to look past me.

"Lil," Mom says, shaking her head with her eyebrows wrinkled together. Mitzy squints and shows me the tip of her tongue because she thinks I'm looking for attention.

When Happy starts barking and trying to climb the front door, Mom wiggles the mistletoe, Mitzy wrestles the dog away, I yank open the door and Mom holds the mistletoe over the Coach's head and jumps up to kiss him on the lips so fast he barely knows what hit him.

"Well," he says, patting down his curly brown moustache and his goatee like he's checking for damage. "Well, that was certainly a surprise."

Mom shakes her head so the bells on her elf cap jingle. "You make my bells ring!"

Mitzy, Davey and I laugh because Mom kisses everybody she can catch under the mistletoe. And she just kissed the cutest teacher in school.

I grab my jacket and follow him out the door. I'm not worried anymore. No one in Acorn Lake ever shot themself—not on purpose. I got carried away. Besides, Randy would never do it before Christmas. He wouldn't do that to Mom. When I get home tonight, I'll fix up the tree a little. Maybe move some ornaments around. I'm always in charge of plugging the bare spots.

. . .

Mitzy said that baby-sitting the four Christian boys is like trying
to herd cats, but every time I stroll from their living room into
their kitchen, I move the clock ahead another fifteen minutes, and
by six o'clock I've got the seven-year-old believing it's eight-
thirty. The kid's not smart. I tell him Santa Claus will shoot right
past their chimney and drop all his toys at the Towneys' next
door if he doesn't get the hell right into bed, and even though
Christmas isn't for eighteen more days, the dummy goes right
up to bed, setting a good example for the other nasty little Christian boys.

I figure at four a.m.—when I'm home in bed—the boys will
be up begging for breakfast, but Mr. C can just coach them back
into bed. You don't disobey a man who coaches football, basketball, wrestling and track. He teaches science too, and math and
art. The walls here are covered with his paintings—mostly five-
foot-tall pink and yellow flowers like puffy lips on long stems.
And there's a bookshelf with trophies and framed pictures of guys
lined up behind Mr. C like they'd follow him anywhere—even
though they're carrying helmets and he's wearing his beret. He's
everybody's favorite, even Randy who quit sports his freshman
year when Mr. C told him he had to make some decisions: deer
hunting or football; crow hunting or basketball; rabbit trapping
or wrestling. The entire year works that way. Randy cleared out
his gym locker and told me he never had to decide a thing
because he just knew.

It's comfortable at the Christians' with his wife at her sister's
and him coaching a game that won't be over until ten. I'm cozy
on the davenport, spending the money in my head. I'll get some
plum-colored wool and have Mom make me an A-line skirt and a
matching vest with wood buttons. She'll sew anything I want.

Later, when Tad Towney knocks on the door, I let him right in. I've been watching TV in the front room with the curtains open, and he's been outside watching me the entire time. Maybe I knew that. You can feel it when someone's watching you. Maybe he was looking for Mitzy. She's dying to go out with him because he's seventeen and six-foot-two, and she's already dated every other boy who comes to school without manure on his shoes.

Tad's never said a word to me before; he's a senior. I get us bottles of Coke, we drink them halfway down, then he fills them with rum he found under the kitchen sink and we sit outside the back door on the cement step in the falling snow, smoking Lucky Strikes from the pack we found in the dresser drawer. He doesn't say a word, so I tell him about Randy and Tuna, talking fast because boys get bored. He shrugs, so I ask him to tell me how to pole-vault. I watch the boys do it in the gym all the time. Tad says girls can't vault because the pole has to slide across your chest—close and fast in one smooth move. "Without anything in the way," he says, like he thinks I don't get it.

"Mitzy could do it."

It's only eight o'clock when Mr. C walks into his den and finds me making out with Tad Towney. Tad's lying on top of me with his hand up my shirt and when he tries to jump to his feet, we tumble off the davenport like two people in one sleeping bag. We unwrap our legs and stand up. I try to catch Tad's eye while Mr. C pushes him in the shoulder, hard, shoving him down the hall sideways. "Hit the road, Tad," he says. "You're done here, Tad." Tad won't look up at me. He's studying his tennis shoes like they're new. He's cute, but he's a coward. He should land on Omaha Beach once.

.   .   .

Mr. C's station wagon is still warm inside. My winter jacket's on over my shirt and skirt, but my bra's still unhooked, giving me that loosey-goosey feeling. You only have to wear one for a couple weeks before you start feeling like parts of you will fall off without it. I'm already bigger than Mitzy.

Mr. C starts the car, jumps out and comes around to my side with the scraper even though it's snowing so softly the wipers could handle it. His first swipe clears a strip of glass, and he's up there looking in at me as he reaches out and pulls back, one long strip at a time, with his curly brown hair poking out of his red beret and his stiff goatee angled straight up by the matching muffler that's wound too tight. The hand with the scraper is red and chapped, but Mr. C's too cool to wear gloves.

As he backs down his driveway with his right arm along the top of the seat and his head turned to see where he's going, his fingers touch my hair and I flinch. I'm still jumpy from Tad.

"Lillian," he says, driving carefully, "you mentioned wanting to pole-vault." He smells like he's had a drink—booze, not beer.

I asked him months ago to teach me how to fling myself off one of those long, springy poles until I'm flipped completely upside down, sailing feet-first straight for the sky. But now all I care about is whether he plans to give me a hard time about Tad. I will refuse to speak. He would never dare tell my father, and Mom would just wink at him because she loves love. Then she'd bug me for details. She always says she's so young for her age you can tell her anything, but we never tell her a thing. I'll bet the Coach liked it when she kissed him. She stands on her head five minutes every day to keep her breasts up where they belong. I see him slide his hand up under her sweater. She leans back so he can give her a long, wet kiss—and I shake my head fast and almost say *ish* out loud. She's not that young.

He says, "I'd be willing to teach you about the art of pole vaulting. For example, were you aware that the Greeks were first to formalize pole vaulting as a competitive sport?"

I hope if I stay quiet, he'll forget about Tad, like it never happened. But I can't think about anything else. I can still feel exactly where his hands touched me, as if the first time a boy touches you in a spot it leaves electric-blue handprints, and everywhere he hasn't touched you yet is still white and shivery—like skin that's waiting. I'm thin, but I have a lot of skin waiting. If Tad weren't such a chicken, I might be head over heels right now. Maybe I just love love. Mr. C's still talking about pole vaulting. And I keep thinking about Tad. If I turn my head to the side I can smell him in my hair. Smoky and sweet. Lucky Strikes and rum. I wonder if the Coach still does it with his wife. She's pink and white and mushy-looking with real long skirts. Mom says you'll find a pair of piano legs under every long skirt, and we say back to her, "If you don't have anything nice to say . . ." and she laughs because she's been caught.

Mr. C says, "Few realize it, of course, but pole vaulting is a three-dimensional art. I prefer to think of it as a kinetic art form, sinuous and fascinating because each jump is utterly unique." He says all this with his beard stuck up in the air, then turns to look me in the eye like he's sure I'm the only one on planet Earth who will understand. He says, "Do you understand, Lillian?" We've turned onto the highway, but his turn signal is still pinging like someone's foot keeping time.

"Uh-huh," I say, wishing he'd be quiet so I could close my eyes and remember what Tad did and imagine what he might have done to me next if Mr. C hadn't interrupted us. We should have started sooner, skipped the cigarettes but maybe not the rum.

"Like snowflakes," Mr. C says, nodding toward the windshield as if I hadn't noticed it's snowing. "Every vault is different from its predecessor. It is perhaps the most beautiful of all the arts."

He clicks the wipers up high because the snow's coming down heavy and wet now. His hard wiper blades are clacking against the glass, and his turn signal is still pinging. In a flash, the inside of the windshield frosts up, he hits his defrosters, and when the hot air follows the curve of the windshield and blows back at me, I lean forward until I'm washing my face and neck in the heat.

He says, "Regardless of the height you achieve, it's never quite high enough."

That's how I always imagine it, like being launched from a slingshot and trying to go as high as I can, trying to make it last, then rolling slowly over the bar, falling until I bounce hard on the mattress. Doing it again. "I'm like that."

"It's human nature, Lillian. It's perfectly natural to want to go higher the next time." His arm is stretched along the top of the seat again. His fingers separate out a strand of my hair and give a little tug, and I shiver hard because it feels as if he touched me everywhere at once. I freeze, hoping he didn't notice. He must have meant it like a pat on the head.

We've crossed the creek and as we're coming up on the Malarkeys' tractor road, the Coach is rubbing the strand of hair between his two fingers, making a crinkly cellophane noise next to my ear. His cold fingernail starts to move along my neck as if he's signing his name. I don't want him to stop, but I don't want him to know what I'm feeling either. I imagine him turning toward me for a kiss. He looks at my face for a long time first. Then his lips are wet and his beard tickles my chin. *Wait,* I think, and I have him use his tongue. Tad used his tongue, so I did too. I picture the Coach pulling off onto the little dirt road under the cottonwood trees where the car might get stuck in the snow, where no one could ever see us. I can see him turning the wheel. Mom always says if you feel something strongly enough, the other person has to feel it too. That's how the world works. I concentrate hard and picture him turning the wheel. I try to feel the wheel turn. *Mr. C, I command you. Turn the wheel.*

He does. And a squeaky "Oh" comes from me.

The tractor road is only used during plowing and planting. It's just two ruts where the tires go. Now it's frozen, and the station wagon bounces so hard I'm grabbing everywhere at once for a handhold. But there's nothing here to hold on to. I fly forward, and barely catch myself in time with my palms flat against the dash. Then it hits me that I should say something. *So stupid.* I should have said something the second he turned the wheel. I could have said, *Kidding!* But I sort of wanted him to and I felt it so strongly that he felt it too. I can't figure out what to say, but the longer you wait the worse it gets. Tuna says girls who lead guys on are cock teasers. Once you say yes, you can't say no.

The Coach forces his way deeper into the lane, ignoring the branches clawing the paint job on his new station wagon and the tearing sound of ruts ripping off his muffler and tailpipe. Even Dad never drives this crazy, not even when he's three sheets to the wind and ready to blow.

The Coach stops the car. He turns off the ignition and sits there perfectly still, facing the windshield with his hand still on the key, not saying a word. Except for the slow tick of the engine cooling, it's quiet now in the dark in the big car with the windows rolled up tight and the leafless cottonwood trees hugging the roof, and the snow falling on top of what's been falling all day like cotton padding all around us, like we're inside a secret where things can happen and it can be like nothing happened at all, like we're inside my head.

He reaches down between his legs and pulls a handle on the floor, and the seat slides back in its tracks with a noise like a freight train coupling miles away, the sound softened by the miles and the snow, everything quiet in the snow.

He turns toward me. Maybe he thinks I know what to do. I want to go home. But I should have said something before he ruined his car for me. If I say something now, he'll explode.

He sets his hands on my shoulders and turns my back toward the door. The cold window shocks the back of my head. My head bumps down the padded door, stops hard on the armrest. My arm is trapped between us. Foot's in the steering wheel. I say, "Wait." But I think he's about to kiss me. I can't say my foot's in the wheel. I say, "Just a second," but not loud. My loafer hangs on the tip of my big toe for a minute. I can't hold it. It falls through the wheel. He turns, reaching back toward my knees, and elbows the rearview mirror, and I see myself, a pale girl looking down on us just before I disappear.

I hear my voice before I feel the pain—dull and muffled like it's miles underground. My head is turned to the side. My eyes are open, but I don't understand what I'm looking at. I blink to make sure my eyes are open. Finally it comes together, the way the snow on the windshield is blurring the moon shining through the bare cottonwood branches. Snow is falling still when the Coach shouts, "I love you," and his head arches back like a runner breaking through the tape.

We're sitting up again. He reaches toward me and I jump. He straightens the hem of my skirt. "Thanks," I say, trying to remember leaving the tractor road. We're almost home when I realize I'm leaking even though it's the wrong time of the month. I sneak my hand behind me to yank down my jacket without him noticing. I'm sitting mostly on it but I still don't know if I'm leaving a stain.

As he turns into our driveway, I begin to open my door. I hold my feet above the moving snow. When he shifts into park, I think to check that I'm wearing both loafers, and I am.

"Lillian," he says, "let me walk you to the door." Like a date. We shouldn't have done that and he knows it. I want to get away from him. No one should ever see us in the same room again. I want to make him promise he'll never tell a soul, but I can't look at him and I can't make myself speak.

The stepping-stones are icy. My legs are shivery. He takes my elbow and I pull away to hurry past the back of the house where six-foot-tall letters made from colored Christmas lights are flashing. LOVE! LOVE! LOVE! Like the EATS! sign at the truck stop. Mom thinks she'll win the decorating contest even though Dad says love isn't a Christmas theme. It embarrasses me now.

Inside our front door, it seems as if Mom drops from the ceiling to kiss the Coach. She backs away smiling, with her shoulders rising, one red sneaker lifting off the floor, and her finger poking up at his face, like someone else is controlling all her body parts. She sings, "You forgot! Mistletoe!" and he looks at the ceiling as if he's checking to make sure it was a fair kiss. And crazy things are running through my head. Offsides. Foul ball. Foot fault. Holding. Kissing. Fucking. I say, "Stop it!" Mom's in her perkiest mood. They must have had a fight, but Dad's still sitting there watching TV. As if my staring woke him up, he says, "Hey-hey, Max!" And he stands up. "How ya doin', Max?"

"Fine and dandy, Jack. Fine and dandy."

I have to get to the bathroom. Mitzy's at the table stringing wire through the wings of an angel, not looking up. Davey's watching. He'll notice if I start backing up the stairs, but he won't say a word.

Mom lifts an armload of Christmas tree lights off the table, tosses a few strands around her shoulders like a shawl, loops others down her arms, leans over, plugs them into the outlet, flips back up, spreads her arms and shouts, "Ta-dahhh!" She's supposed to be a cross. "Another Masterpiece by Marion!"

Mr. C backs away from her as if he thinks she's strange. I want to say it's just Christmas. That she's like this just to make Christmas for us. He reaches out to shake Dad's hand, and when their skin touches, it feels as if everything in the room should light up with everybody knowing what happened in the station wagon. How could they not know? I'm standing right here.

But the TV's still on too loud, Mom's checking her shoulder for loose bulbs, Davey's raking his fingers through a clump of tinsel, and Mitzy's looking at the angel, turning it over in her hands. Mr. C smiles at the top of her head and says, "Hi, Mitzy," then nods at each of us in turn. "Good baby-sitters." Nobody heard, but it's like the windshield got wiped. He hands me some dollar bills. "Have to run. My boys are home alone."

I'm in the bathroom with the door locked, lying in a tub of hot water up to the top of my sealed lips. I drain the tub, fill it, drain it, fill it. It's as if I've been varnished wherever he touched me. I've been stained. I shampoo my hair. I scrub my skin raw with a washrag. There's no place I haven't been touched. I fling the washrag and it hits the mirror with a splat.

I dress in clean clothes, put my jacket back on, and find Tuna,

Randy and Davey in the boys' room. I sit on the empty bed against the corner of the wall, wet hair in a towel, legs folded under me, jacket zipped tight, thumbs in my fists, fists in my sleeves, messy bedspread tucked under my armpits. I always sit in here reading a book while Randy flips through *Sports Afield* or *Bowhunter*, neither of us saying a thing. Every now and then we look at each other and smile.

Tuna's kneeling on the other bed next to Davey, naming the parts of the Playboy Bunny on the foldout nailed to the wall. He says the best girls all have staples in their navels. Randy's sitting on the end of the bed, cleaning a number four rabbit trap with the WD-40.

Mitzy appears in the doorway and stands there staring at me and looking pissed off. I turn away, hoping she doesn't want to fight about anything.

Randy says, "But if we both shoot ourselves in the foot, they're not going to believe it's an accident." After a second he shakes his head. "They'd probably make us go anyway. We'd have to crutch our way through the jungle." He sets the rabbit trap aside, stands up and limps in a quick circle, almost falling over when his crutch sinks in the mud.

Tuna lights up. "Hey! We could shoot opposite feet so it's not so obvious." Then he says they could really get away with it if they picked completely different body parts—say he shot his foot and Randy shot his hand, maybe even a couple days apart.

Mitzy walks toward me and sits on the bed, then scoots back until we're sitting next to each other, touching from elbow to shoulder, both of us up as tight as we can be against the wall. I cross my arms and tuck my hands into my armpits. Mitzy does the same and our fingertips touch. We stay like that.

Davey slides off the bed onto the floor, leans against the wall with his knees pulled up to his chest, and stares up at Randy while Randy and Tuna argue about what would be worse: losing a foot or losing a hand. Finally they agree the left hand would be the thing to give up because you'd still have two feet for walking into the woods to go hunting, and you could train yourself to balance the rifle barrel on your left wrist while you hold the butt tight to your shoulder and pull the trigger with your right index finger. They try it out with pretend rifles, laughing and shouting "Pow! Pow! Pow!"

Finally Randy says, "What the heck. We're never going to do anything. We'll just sit here and let it all happen to us. We'll just let it happen."

Tuna's still laughing, bouncing around like he's on fire. "Yeah," he says, and punches Randy's shoulder, one quick jab, "but at least then if we get killed, it won't be our fault." He falls to one knee and with an imaginary rifle at his hip, he sprays the room with bullets, finishing us all off.

Randy laughs and goes back to his rabbit trap. Mitzy starts sucking air through her teeth. Davey puts his elbows on his knees, crosses his arms and drops his head in.

I think about it for a long time. Finally I say, "Yes, it will."

1966

Duck Season

My sister is the kind of girl who thinks letting Buddy Franklin fuck her in the Hoffmans' hayloft is the same thing as a date. Now she's over on the Franklins' double-wide dock in her orange bikini, sitting with half a dozen rich Minneapolis girls who smear their long, thin legs with coconut suntan lotion while the Franklin boys show off slalom skiing behind their new jet boat. It's a candy-apple-green fiberglass job with a ninety-horse inboard-outboard Johnson powerful enough to pull four skiers up out of the water in under fourteen seconds. Mitzy goes over there every day after her shift at the Minnewashka Pickle Factory where lots of Acorn Lake kids have summer jobs.

Normally I know enough to keep away from city kids, but we're alone out here from September to June, sixty miles from Minneapolis, five miles past town, hip-high in snowdrifts, with the summer cabins boarded up around us like the party's over. And this summer Randy's five hours north of here, rolling sod for a buck an hour—like the draft board can't find Bemidji. I invite Happy into the fishing boat and row to the Franklins', where I stay in the boat, at eye level with the dock, fingers loose around the dock pole so no one thinks I care enough to stay.

A brunette girl with turquoise eyes and a matching towel is tinkering with a transistor radio, trying to find WDGY Rock and Roll. "You girls live out here *all* year-round?" Polka music flares, but she dials it away and finds "Summer in the City." She cranks up the volume. *Hot town, summer in the city, back of my neck . . .* There are tiny yellow ruffles on her shoulder straps. I wonder how much that suit cost.

"Yup," Mitzy says, lying on her stomach, knees bent, waving her feet around like bait.

"You even go to school out here?"

Happy jumps from the boat and sits on the edge of Mitzy's towel like a traitor.

"Lots of people do," I say.

"Locals," Buddy Franklin says. He's standing waist-deep in the water, drinking a bottle of beer, one elbow on the side of his boat like we might forget who owns it. I saw Buddy and Rollie roar into their driveway this morning in their dad's new station wagon, bringing out a load of girls for the weekend. Everyone says Buddy's handsome, but he's got squinty eyes. "Locals," he says again, nodding toward Henry Hoffman who's riding shotgun in the boat, wearing long sleeves, black trousers and heavy street shoes. His folks lease the farm across the hill. People say he was born a bubble off of plumb. He's been a sophomore for years.

Mitzy sits up, drops her straps and rubs baby oil over her shoulders and down where the cleavage would be if she weren't flat as a barn door. She holds her shoulders back and puckers her fleshy lips, staring at Buddy, her short blond hair combed back into a ducktail like she thinks every inch of her face deserves to show. I leave mine long so I can pull it like a curtain. Blushing is the curse of redheads.

A blonde sitting next to Mitzy lifts a knee and slides her hand to the back of her calf to feel the muscle ride up when she arches her bare foot. Girls like her think no one is smart enough to see what they're doing. "But where do you shop?" she asks.

I'm wearing my good tan Bermudas and the tangerine-colored blouse Mom made for me. "In the *city*." I cross my legs. I arch my foot. I look thin in this outfit. "We shop in the city."

"No way," Mitzy says. "I sew my own clothes." It's true. She won the Singer Sewing Machine contest for her original design of a blouse with a Peter Pan collar. At the awards ceremony, the judges raved about her bust darts and the hundreds of tiny blind stitches Mom taught her to use for hems. They gave her a portable sewing machine. I refuse to sew.

The waves are making little licking noises against the ski boat, and the sun's reflecting off the aluminum trim. The temperature and the humidity are both near ninety.

Rollie's sitting on the bow, flexing his pecs, one side at a time. I'm counting four beats to a side when I realize Mitzy's warning all of them never to eat Minnewashka pickles because the night shift guys piss in the brine vats if the supervisor won't give them an extra bathroom break. Mitzy's on her feet, using every inch of her half-naked body to act it out, spit flying like popcorn while the city girls look at each other, smiling calm little rich-girl smiles.

I pull the cord on our little Evinrude, mutter *Thank you, God!* when it starts and race away without looking back.

On the other side of the bay, I push way back into the creek, finally slowing to a putter in the reedy shallows where the swamp begins. I turn the motor off, tilt it up and slip the oars into the locks. After a couple strokes, I sit still in all the greenness, watching purple dragonflies crash-land on the watery mirror, watching half-crazed crappies break the surface to grab gnats, while all the insects buzz in one high-pitched note. Everything is swollen and wet. I glide back out and follow the ragged outline of the lake, the dry wooden oars scraping gently against my damp palms. Near the point, the tops of boulders seem to flake away as rock-colored mud turtles slither into the water. I start the motor and work my way around the edge of the lake to the far side where there isn't room to wedge a cabin between the steep shore and the gravel road.

In the soft shadows of the overhanging willow trees, a mallard hen is swimming with nine ducklings lined up behind her like they're strung together on monofilament line. Much as you want to, you can't just grab a wild duck, so I sit back on the transom to steer with one hand and lean over the water with the long-handled fishing net in the other. The hen lifts up, then remembers her ducklings can't fly yet and swings around to land behind them, quacking loud as the motor. She herds them away from me under her wings, but I pull slightly past them, slow down, turn sharp and cut them off. While they're bumping the side of the boat, I push the net down into the water and scoop up a wiggling, quacking baby mallard. You have to love a baby duck. The next hour is a water rodeo. I leave the hen with four ducklings, figuring she won't remember the rest for long.

I'm heading home when the motor conks. I check the bubble gauge on the gas can. I pump the fuel line. I pull the rope handle thirty times, then thirty more before removing the housing to work my way back through every oily connection. Meanwhile, I drift. I'm rubbing grease off my knee when the rumble of another small motor interrupts me.

A long wooden fishing boat's coming at me from the shore of an old trapper's cabin that sits alone on the only solid piece of land in a swamp stretching back into miles of peat bog full of snakes and snapping turtles. The boat's being driven by a skinny shirtless guy with thick black hair blowing back from a high forehead. He pulls alongside me, then leans closer when he sees the ducklings trying to waddle up the sides of my boat, crapping long white streams. He laughs. Then I do too because nothing craps like a scared duck.

"Need help?" He might be twenty.

"Nope."

With his free hand he clamps the two boats together. He has small bright-blue eyes under thick black eyebrows. He doesn't look like anyone from here. He's dark tan and his face is craggy, with deep dimples running straight down both sides and under his handlebar moustache.

I hope I don't have grease on my face. I cross my legs and arch my foot.

"Where abouts do you live?" he asks, propping a booted foot on the side of his boat. Nobody wears cowboy boots in a fishing boat.

I point two miles across the lake to where our house is a brown speck dead center in the smallest bay. "Who're you, anyway?" I ask.

"Larry."

"You're not the trapper."

"He's dead. Know him?"

"Not anymore."

He looks surprised.

"Just kidding," I say. "Nobody did."

I let Larry tow me across the lake.

I put the ducks in the wire rabbit pen by the road. It's been empty since we ate the rabbits in the early spring. *Those rabbits multiply like rabbits,* Mom kept saying, wiggling her eyebrows. She thinks anything that even hints at sex is funny. *Sexual innuendo,* she'll say, moving her lips over the words as if she's talking to a deaf person. Phrases from her year of high school French only come back to her in public places. *I'll have a cut-up fryer. With the giblets, see boo play.* I've stopped going anywhere with her—which is just as well because Davey lives in the passenger seat of her car like the eight-year-old *TV Guide* on our coffee table. He cried for two years after he was born and so did I.

The idea of eating your own rabbits would send the Franklins' girlfriends running, but like Dad keeps telling me, Acorn Lake farm kids have to raise an animal a year for 4-H—a calf or a hog, something big—just to practice not falling in love with what they'll have to butcher right after the county fair. Dad says eating a bunch of rabbits shouldn't have been such a big goddamn deal. It caught me off guard is all because they were white and I didn't think we ate white rabbits.

I feed the ducks some bread, leave them a dishpan of water, and go to bed that night thinking about how to dig a pond in the pen. If you keep ducklings penned up and well fed, they never learn to fly. I could even line the pond with plastic and make a rock border. An island might be possible.

At midnight I climb out the hall window onto the flat section of the roof and sit there a long time, staring at the only light on the other side of the lake.

Early next morning I clean the plugs in the motor, and Happy and I go across to the trapper's cabin where Larry's putting his wooden rowboat upside down on two sawhorses in his weedy mess of a lawn. I beach my boat, sit in the shade under the lilac bushes and watch.

"How are those ducks?" he asks.

"Fine." I bury my nose in lilacs and inhale until the taste of purple nearly makes me cry.

He scrapes long, skinny strips of green paint off the boat. "Not planning to eat those little ducks, are you?"

I shake my head. "That's why I have to name them."

He lights a cigar stub and leans against his boat, squinting at me through yellow smoke, waiting to hear more.

"We've never eaten anything that had a name."

"And what *nameless* things have you eaten?"

"Rabbits mostly. Well . . . deer, elk, pheasants, ducks, grouse, geese, turtles. Ate some bear once. Mom says, *If it moves, Dad shoots it.*"

He blows a smoke ring and folds himself down onto the grass as if he's hinged like Dad's camping stool. He watches me. He's waiting to hear more.

"And fish. Dad filleted my pet Northern. Ten-pounder I speared in the creek. Got him just in the tail, so he was fine in the bathtub when I left for school."

He licks the finger and thumb of one hand and smoothes down his moustache. He's shirtless and barefoot, jeans sitting low on his skinny hips. "Eat him?"

"Yeah. My rabbits too. Except the ones still in the freezer."

Larry doesn't have much hair on his chest. "Dog got a name?"

I nod. "Dinner." It's an old joke, but he's never heard it. I like the way he laughs without making a lot of noise, as if it's only for him.

Larry and I name the mallards Alexandra, Amanda, Josephine, Mary Louise and Elizabeth, after two queens, he says, and three of his old girlfriends. He gives me a flat piece of wood, a can of white paint and a small brush, and I make a sign for the rabbit pen while he works on his boat.

"I'm gonna pitch the tent in the backyard," Mitzy says. She takes a bottle of the new Diet Pepsi from the refrigerator and rolls it across the tan skin between the top and bottom of her bikini. "Way too hot to sleep in the house."

"Fine, honey." Mom's standing on the kitchen counter, barefoot and tan in short shorts and a pink halter top, hanging a row of Shell No-Pest Strips in front of a torn window screen. Her test run's still hanging above the table, looking like it was dipped in flies. I'd rather have a hundred flies dive-bombing me than eat breakfast staring at a strip of them half dead, half still squirming. *Buzzzzzzzz*ing. If they could learn to cry like babies, no one would ever buy another Shell No-Pest Strip.

Davey's sitting on the counter in cutoffs, drumming his heels against the cupboard doors.

"Me too," I say. "I'm sleeping in the tent."

Mom nods and pushes another tack into the window frame.

Mitzy gives me the look. "You're such an atheist." Like atheists sleep in tents.

I tap my temple with my finger, turn my back so Mom can't hear, and hiss, "At least I don't put out for every boy in town."

"Who'd want you? You're turning into a tub."

"Mitzy," Mom says, "be kind. Your sister's just fighting off a little baby fat."

I was always naturally thin until I woke up pudgy on Christmas morning. Mom says it's from spending all my time in bed, under the covers, mowing through books and ripple chips. I'm either there or in the bathtub.

She jumps down off the counter. "Sure do love my kids."

Mitzy says, "Love you too."

I say, "Love you."

Davey says, "Love you."

I knew it. At midnight Mitzy and I are lying in our shortie summer nightgowns on top of sleeping bags in the mildewed canvas umbrella tent. It's hot and humid, and we're listening to a billion crickets when someone walks across the crushed gravel driveway in bare feet. Buddy Franklin doesn't have the brains to stay on the grass. Henry Hoffman has to be out there somewhere too, trailing Buddy, picking up city boy skills, but even Henry's smart enough to stay on the grass, and he disappears in the dark.

I wait until Mitzy unties the mosquito flap over the door. "Hah!" I say, sitting up, pointing a finger. "Hah!"

"Oh, shut up." She slips out and leaves the flap open. Happy follows, wagging her tail like it's a hunting trip.

A few minutes later I go after them. I reach the road in time to see two shadows holding hands, running through the field for another one of their dates. This time I don't follow.

I wander to the shore and sit on the dock. I can't see Larry's light across the lake. I look back through our picture window at the flickering glow from the TV and fight the urge to make sure

Dad hasn't fallen asleep with a lit cigarette. I've almost broken the habit of getting up every few hours at night to check, but I keep seeing the house burst into flames and I know it's my fault for not stopping it when I had the chance.

Dad walks past the window carrying something in either hand, probably a beer and the dill pickle jar. He'll sit up all night, drinking his way through a case of beer, crunching pickles with a sound like his head's hollow. Then he'll drink the brine from the jar, even though the doctor said it fertilizes stomach ulcers. Dad's are growing back, but Mitzy keeps bringing him free pickles.

I steer clear of Dad. Mom says I have a talent for saying the one thing that'll launch him. Like *good morning,* or *hello.*

I take the boat to Larry's every day. He bought the cabin and everything in it for back taxes after the trapper died. We paint his boat. We mow the scraggly lawn and throw grass seed around. We dig a fire pit to grill the largemouth bass I catch under the willows using the tiniest frogs Larry says he's ever seen. (The secret's hooking them under the chin so they still wiggle their legs. You want lively bait.) We eat butterscotch candies by the bag, and I pretend to like the Coors he brought from Colorado.

By mid-July, my ducks are so fat I prop the pen open with a brick and they walk out quacking, rocking side to side the way ducks do because they don't have knees. They start spending their time swimming around the docks in our bay. When their feathers grow out, I rename Josephine and Elizabeth, calling them Joe and Larry.

Larry—the original Larry—teaches me how to smoke cigars. "The biggest mistake a girl can make," he says, sitting on the cabin's wooden front steps, "is inhaling hard just because some guy hands them his cigar. With a fine Cuban cigar, you just puff soft, then exhale." We spend days trying to blow square smoke rings. He knows an Apache in Provo, Utah, who could do it every time. Larry inherited a few bucks, he says, when his dad died, and spent most of it traveling the world, meeting fascinating people. "Like you," he says. He teaches me to say Zihuatanejo *(zee-wah-tin-ay-ho)*. Ixtapa. Okeechobee. He tells me about Ketchikan and the Monongahela. Baton Rouge. Pensacola.

Mitzy and I have been sleeping in the tent most of the summer. No matter how strange a thing is, if it happens twice at our house, it becomes normal—like the gutters balanced on bricks in the grass around the edge of the house. We step over them, not thinking anymore about how they should be nailed to the eaves instead of waiting below to catch the runoff.

Nights in the backyard become normal. And if you ask where I am all day, Mom will say *fishing,* not noticing I've been fishing for thirty-four straight days and have never brought home a fish. She knows I can take care of myself.

The first night Mitzy brings Buddy into the tent, I don't say a word, lying on my stomach in my sleeping bag in the dark. Listening to them kiss and moan gets me rocking on my hand, thinking what it would be like with Larry. I'm minding my own business when Buddy shouts, "I love you. Holy Christ, Mitzy, I really love you."

I sit right up. "You're such a slut . . . just a stupid slut. How can you believe him? Just *stupid . . .*" I jump up, not looking their way because I saw more of them than I ever wanted to, standing on the top rung of the ladder, peeking into Hoffmans' hayloft in the early spring.

"Shut up," Mitzy says. "Just shut up."

Scrambling out of the tent, I scrape my leg on the metal stake holding the door flap open. Happy follows as I limp to the lake and stand on the beach. The light breeze blows the cool wet patch on my nightgown against my thigh. I look back at the flickering TV in the window, then turn and push the boat out with the long hiss of aluminum on sand. Happy swims after me, but I row away. In the middle of the bay I start the noisy motor. Happy's smart enough to turn around.

Larry's light doesn't come on when I pound. He just opens his door in his underwear and stands back to let me in as if I come here every night. He pulls on his jeans, lights a candle and tosses me a shirt to put over my nightgown before he washes out the cut on my leg.

We're sitting on the end of the dock in the starlight when he kisses me, tickling my lips with his moustache, tasting like a fine Cuban cigar and the tequila and lime he's been teaching me about. Only our faces touch. Then he turns forward again. "I like you a lot," he says. I nod. I lick salt off my lips, looking across the lake toward our house, checking for fire. But everything's dark. I slip off the shirt he gave me and ease down into the lake until I'm weightless, my nightgown floating up around me like egg white cooking on dark water. Larry gets up. He stands on the dock, smoothing down his moustache, thinking while he shifts his weight from one foot to the other, watching me. Finally he pulls his jeans and his underwear off his long legs and slips himself quietly into the lake.

Treading water nose to nose, we're laughing like babies in a bathtub. He says again, "I like you, Lillian."

"I know." I'm sure it's the truth because I learned to keep my ears perked for lies, learned it from the Coach just before

Christmas—learned that and how to say *no* sooner. I said it, but I said it too late. Now I can smell a lie before a guy even thinks it. So I don't have to give it up. I just won't do it with a boy who lies, and I'll never do it with a boy who isn't a friend of mine.

The next afternoon I find Larry packing up his big red Pontiac, heading out for Zihuatanejo. I'm not surprised. You can fish there all winter, buy a bag of clams from a beach kid for thirty-five cents. You can live for two dollars a day, so Larry won't have to get a job for another year. Maybe longer.

He gives me a frozen Folger's Coffee can, says there's a mink pelt preserved inside, kisses me on the forehead and says he'll see me in the spring. After he drives away, I sit on his front steps for a while, thinking. Finally I lift the aluminum foil lid off the can. I can see the spot where he scraped the ice off the shiny brown fur. The mink pelt might have been frozen in this can for years.

On opening day of duck season it's quiet on the lake because all the summer kids are gone and lake kids are born knowing not to play near the water in the fall when hunters hide behind blinds with their thick shotguns loaded and their safeties off. The law says you can't fire a shot before noon, so at nine a.m. I start rowing across the bay with the fishing net to herd Larry, Joe, Alexandra, Amanda and Mary Louise back home into their pen. Happy lopes along the beach, barking at me. She was chasing the mailman's car when I was ready to leave, but I should've waited.

I turn and see the ducks from a distance, paddling around a dock where there's always duckweed. Halfway there, rowing slow and steady, I turn again and see Henry Hoffman walking onto the dock in long sleeves, long pants and heavy black shoes, with his shotgun resting inside his bent elbow. At the end of the dock he bends down on one knee, and the ducks race to be first to get fed, paddling wildly, running over each other, using their wings like clumsy oars because they never learned to fly. Ducks aren't smart. I row as fast as I can, angling the boat so I can see. The one out front has to be Mary Louise; she's half again as big as the rest. Henry stands up, stamps on the dock, and when they don't fly away, he settles the butt of his shotgun against his shoulder. "No," I scream, "no," like in those dreams where you scream and solid white silence shoots from your mouth. Henry aims down at Mary Louise. He pulls the trigger. She jumps a little—as if he only startled her—and then she collapses. Happy's running along the beach full-out now, barking so hard it looks like she's eating air. The sound of the gun thrills her.

Henry swivels to the right and shoots another duck. Then another, then another.

I shout, "Don't." I shout, "No. No. Please. Don't."

Henry aims at the last duck as Happy corners onto the long wooden dock. *Bark! Bark! Bark!* Racing toward Henry. The gun fires. *Bark! Bark!* My dog's going to fetch my dead ducks—doesn't matter who feeds the dog every morning or who kills the ducks or whether they have names. Happy races past Henry, throws herself off the dock, legs paddling before she hits the water. Fucking dog. Dead ducks are in the water, and Happy will do what she was born to do. I only wish she wouldn't do it right in front of me.

She takes a limp dead duck in her soft mouth, dog-paddles back and delivers it to Henry on the sand, then does it four more times while I sit in the boat a hundred yards offshore, struck stupid, wondering only how Henry's going to carry my ducks. I see myself beaching the boat at full speed and leaping out to shove him in the chest with both hands. I knock him over and claim the bodies. But you don't bury dead ducks. Not if they're fresh you don't. I'd end up cleaning the damn things.

I put the motor down, make a U-turn and follow the curve of the bay. Mom and Mitzy are standing on the end of our dock with Davey behind them, fists on their hips, heads pushed forward, not believing anyone would take a shot before noon—even though Dad's the biggest poacher in Sioux County. But they'd have heard the shots. Everything is louder when you live on the edge of a lake. Mom tries to wave me in, but I stay far enough out so they can't see I'm crying. I don't want anybody ever looking at me like the girl who got her ducks shot.

Way back where the creek turns to swamp, I shut off the motor and pull myself from bog to bog on the long yellow grass, breathing in the cold orange quiet of fall and finally wedging the bow of the boat into the reeds. In the spring I'll tell Larry about all of this. I slip off the seat and lie crossways, cradled in the bottom of the boat, staring at the pale sky. Rivets dig into my shoulders and hips, but the aluminum boat gives back some of the warmth from the sun while I tell Larry the whole story, over and over, watching his face to know where to change it for the next time. A couple hours later I'm explaining how I shoved Henry so hard he fell backward onto the sand like a tree into a ditch. Larry will laugh when I say it: *like a tree into a ditch.* I'm standing over Henry, pointing his own shotgun into his face. I've got the sight bead lined up perfectly when the real shooting starts in the distance, big *POPS!* from the shotguns. And I sit up to leave, because even Mitzy knows better than to trust a bunch of hunters back in the creek after duck season opens.

The Gift

*I*n the living room at four a.m., I'm crouched in the clutter of Dad's half-packed hunting gear, sneaking chocolate-covered peanuts from his ice chest, when he shouts from upstairs, "Marion? Where'd you put my damn socks?" But Mom's where she always is—in the driveway trying to jump-start her De Soto from his Cadillac.

He stomps downstairs in his boxer shorts, hoping to look like a man whose wife won't launder his clothes—and nearly trips over the neatly folded undershirts on the fourth step and the clean socks on the fifth. "Where the hell's your mother?" Like someone took her. He always thinks people are stealing his things. *Where's my* TV Guide, *where's that box of shotgun shells, where the hell's my dinner?*

I shrug big and whisper to the wall through a mouthful of chocolate-covered peanuts, "Beauty parlor, Jack. Your wife is at the beauty parlor." I reach deep into his ice chest and separate out six more. No one's allowed to eat Dad's peanuts. They're expensive. I'll stop after four more, maybe five, but only because Randy says my hips are growing so fast it's like watching my center of gravity fall.

Dad looks around at the mess Mom always makes when she's packing him up. In one hour he and Randy are leaving for the final duck-hunting trip before Randy reports to boot camp. I'd rather be fifteen and chunky than nineteen, newly drafted, looking at thirteen days of freedom, six weeks of boot camp and a year in Vietnam. We've been not talking about it for months. We don't say Vietnam, Vietcong, casualty, body bag, body count, Huey, hand grenade or jungle. We don't say drafted. We don't say shit. We never read the paper anyway, and we've stopped watching the evening news.

Mom and Randy come in the side door. Without noticing Dad, Randy yanks off his cap and ten inches of yellow hair leap out like snakes, startling Dad who shouts, "Jesus Christ! Jesus Christ!" with his hands fluttering in front of his face. You'd think he hadn't already screamed about every inch of hair that's grown on Randy's head since he finished high school last year. His hair is longer than the Beatles'. Dad's looking at him as if he were just born: Zap! There you have it. A six-foot-four-inch son, the only Anderson ever to top five-nine. "I'm not going hunting with some kid who looks like Jayne Mansfield."

My brother is a hundred and ninety-seven pounds of tempered steel. He taught me to say that. Mom always says it's no wonder Uncle Sam wants him; he's God's gift to women—as if Uncle Sam only takes what women want. Now she says in her gooey voice—I hate her gooey voice—"Darling, we've been all through this. Randy promised he'd keep his hair hidden in his cap the entire time he's with you. Before you know it, you won't even remember."

Randy tucks his hair behind his ears. He can keep his face plain as a slab of cheese for days when Dad's on his case.

Mitzy comes down the stairs, followed by Davey. Nobody around here sleeps at night, but we nap like crazy. Since Mitzy turned seventeen, she's been wearing a black baby-doll pajama top and underpants outfit from the minute she gets home from school. Piss my sister off and she could chew the tires off your car, but when she sees Dad's face in a knot, she freezes. Davey stops behind her, arms going limp in their sockets, looking harmless so no one will confuse him with some nine-year-old with the guts to pick a side. Why this family needed another baby when I was already six, I'll never know and they'll never say.

Dad spins around, taking in each of us like he's trying to figure out who we are—Randy and Mom by the door, Mitzy and Davey on the steps, me beside the ice chest. Never corner a man who has a hair trigger. (That's Randy's joke.) Dad steps toward Mom. "You're gonna cut his goddamned hair."

"Jack . . ."

"What did I just say?"

Randy starts to move between them, but when Mom's eyes close and her lips peel back from her tiny teeth, even Dad pauses. She says in a low voice, "You're leaving, Jack." Then her eyes pop open, and she's all over the room like a wind-up toy, zipping sleeping bags, tying up gunnysacks of wooden decoys, topping off the ice chest with sandwiches and bottles of beer until suddenly all of Dad's stuff is at the door, wrapped and zipped and folded, tied up, tucked in, packed, ready to go. And he's standing there in his boxer shorts looking surprised.

.　　.　　.

Randy and Dad are hardly gone when Mom flies up the stairs and dives into the hall closet no one ever opens because there's nothing in there you'd ever want to see again—which is true of every closet in our house. We have a lot of stuff, but it's all the wrong stuff.

"Just stand there," she says to Mitzy, Davey and me as she struggles out from behind the hanging clothes, tugging on a perfectly cut, heavy white cardboard sign, maybe two feet by three, hand-lettered in black: NEED A GIFT FOR THE WIFE??

"What?" I ask. "What?" But she's back in the closet. I know everything that goes on in this house. None of it has a thing to do with me, but I pay attention. "Hey. Mom."

The next sign says: WE'VE GOT THE KNIFE.

"Davey? Did you know about this?"

"I did not," he says, like he's in court. In the nine long years since he was born, he's never let a single wrong word slip through his lips. The kid barely breathes.

"Mitzy?"

She's leaning against our bedroom door frame, sliding up and down, scratching her back. "Nope."

Mom's holding a sign: CHAIN SAW SHOT? HERE'S THE SPOT!!!!

An hour later we've lined the signs up against the outside of the garage in the order Mom wants them. The temperature has risen to thirty-seven, melting the snow, leaving the backyard like a straw doormat. Mom skips past me, a blond pixie in short sleeves and Bermudas. She wiggles her eyebrows. "So, Lily Nilly. So, so, so?"

There are fifteen signs:

- NEED A GIFT FOR THE WIFE??
- WE'VE GOT THE KNIFE.
- SATURDAY. ALL DAY!
- NEED A PAIL BUT CAN'T MAKE BAIL?
- 4 MORE MILES TO MARION'S SALE.
- HOLD IT, WILL YOU? PLEASE SLOW DOWN!!!
- JACK'S OUT OF TOWN!!!!!!!!
- MONEY TO BURN?
- TAKE THIS TURN!
- NEED A DRILL BUT CAN'T PAY THE BILL?
- MARION IS DOWN THE HILL!
- NEED A GIFT TONIGHT? TAKE A RIGHT!!
- SMILE BOYS SMILE!!
- JUST ONE MORE MILE!!
- CHAIN SAW SHOT? HERE'S THE SPOT!!!!

Mom calls me sneaky just because I don't have to announce my life like a football game. But I'm not sneaky. Not compared to her.

The first Monday of every month for eighteen years the Fargo headquarters of the Handy Hardware Wholesale Company has shipped samples to our house with a mimeograph of the same dateless Dear Sales Employee letter saying Dad should demonstrate the new products at each store he calls on, then sell the samples to one of them at a demo price. Instead he drops them on the stepping-stones, the dining room table or the floor in front of the toilet next to his open *Field and Stream,* and Mom hauls them to the garage—which is why the mess is hers; if she hadn't put all that shit in there, he says, then there would be room for her car. Then he reminds her it's not good to let your car sit outside, especially in the winter.

Every March after months of shoveling and jump-starting, after the first false spring when the melting and refreezing have frozen Mom's tires to the driveway, sometime during the first half of the state basketball–finals blizzard, she loses it. For days she weeps, he shouts, she begs, he shouts, she threatens to walk, he threatens to walk first, she threatens suicide, he promises to sell his samples, she believes him and the next day she's toting new samples to the garage, happy as a Munchkin because he finally loves her enough to change.

Mitzy, Davey and I skip school Thursday and Friday. We nail signs to fence posts and trees along the five miles between our house and downtown Acorn Lake. When Mom says we can pick the one thing we've always wanted most, we rifle Dad's samples. She stops working long enough to choose an electric shaver in its own pink flip-top case. Mitzy will graduate and move out in the spring, so she grabs a waffle iron still in a box with a Handy Hardware letter dated May 1955, It's older than the De Soto. Hell, it's older than Davey who's holding up the eight-inch switchblade with a real horn handle that Randy always wanted. Randy asked once if he could keep it, but Dad said it was worth a lot. So he's been sneaking it for years—using it, cleaning it, putting it back. Mom smiles at Davey. "Why don't you give it to Randy?"

Mitzy says, "Where he's going, it could come in handy." I'd give her the evil eye, but her face is still in the waffle iron box. Mom claps her hands. "Busy, busy, busy."

We tape price tags to everything else. Mom holds up a shovel or a paper sack full of ten-penny nails. "Two dollars?" We say yes. I choose a light-up cosmetic mirror and a branches-and-vines camouflage cap so good that if he drops it in the jungle, it'll never be found again.

At ten a.m. Saturday the temperature hits fifty-eight, setting an all-time Sioux County duck season high. Up and down our dirt road the sun is glinting off parked cars and trucks. And just inside the open garage door Mom is sitting at the card table wearing high heels, red pants and her red sweater over her pointy bra. She's guarding two cake pans full of money. When cantaloupe is your favorite food, it's easy to weigh a hundred and eight.

Bung Gunderson showed up this morning before we were out of bed. He keeps bringing stuff to the table, dragging his bad leg across the oily floor. "Mine," he says. "Mine, mine, mine—" Like Lazy Acres Beach and Campground and all the land north of the lake.

Joe Hearse buys the entire chipboard display of tiny paint cans and all the brushes I priced at twenty-five cents apiece. I should have said fifty. So I sell him *Gearhardt's Guide to Lip-Squeaking for Varmints,* a decent crow call and a Coleman lantern missing a piece of glass.

Coach Christian buys the lawn mower that sat there all summer while ours was broken. His wife stands in front of him looking hopeful and fragile as always, except she's clutching a twenty-five-pound box with a Deluxe Sunbeam Mixmaster mixer in harvest gold that came with an extra set of beaters and three glass bowls. He makes her wait. Finally he nods. She squeals and sprints toward their station wagon with her pink hair bow bouncing off her head. He calls, "But it's for your birthday."

Why would anyone get married? I should've sold her the Luger in the felt-lined wooden box with the brass-hinged lid. Hell, I should've given it to her.

When Natasha Kahout from my grade shows up with her father, I feel a tidal wave of relief that I put the light-up mirror in my bedroom. He'd have bought it for her and she'd have worked it into our conversations every day until we graduate from high school. There's a Kahout in every grade—all the girls are goody-goody cheerleaders, hipless girls wearing flippy skirts in school colors. I always tell Natasha that maroon just isn't her color. Now she's peeking into every box, trying to look bored. I stand against the wall. I am bored.

At one-thirty Walleye Watson, owner of the Acorn Lake Hardware Store, comes through like Sherlock Holmes, turning over price tags, checking style numbers, walking with his head slung forward as if he's climbing a hill. He starts scooping up power tools: a sander, a saw, a drill, a fancy electric screwdriver set. He stacks them next to Mom and sticks his face into hers. "Does Jack know about this?"

Mom's eyes glitter. "It's sort of a surprise."

"What the heck is going on here?"

"I'm clearing a space for myself." She stands up and points where the cement floor would be if it weren't buried under boxes. "I need six feet three inches by fourteen feet nine and a half inches."

Walleye's staring at her.

"I can't spend another winter taking turns with Randy, getting up every two hours in the middle of the night to go outside and run my car for fifteen minutes so the oil doesn't freeze." She's rubbing the shivers out of her arms. She stops, wide-eyed, as if she realized all over again that Randy won't be here. She shakes her head and her eyes refocus.

"I can understand that," Walleye says slowly. "But you can't sell an unused Black and Decker Model 35 Deluxe Power Saw unopened in its original box with two attachments at a garage sale for four dollars and ninety-nine cents."

She explains that she priced everything low on purpose so it would sell. She winks. "Four ninety-nine is really five dollars."

I vow I will never wink.

"You are undercutting my prices," he says.

"Walleye, you've owned a store all your life. Like your dad and his dad . . ."

"For God's sake. You have more inventory than I do."

"But I've only got today."

"I'm running a business."

"I'm having a garage sale."

He shakes a power drill in her face. "I am Jack's best customer. You live off the commission he makes selling hardware to me."

She smiles.

He hisses. "Let me explain: You're going to sell this to one of those guys"—he looks around the crowded garage—"for five bucks."

"Four ninety-nine."

"Four ninety-nine. Which means he won't come in to buy one from me for twenty-seven fifty. Which also means he won't buy impulse items from my front counter. Awwww, Marion, you don't even know what an impulse item is." He says it with his elbow resting on a sign: BATTERIES!!!!! KEEP YOUR LIFE

HUMMING!! Davey made the sign and stuck it in a garbage pail he'd filled with every battery he could find.

Walleye waves the power drill at our customers. "Marion. Look. Can you see what you're doing?" He leans close and whispers, "What's wrong with you?"

Mom's eyes get wide like she's been found out.

He pats her shoulder. "Honey"—she likes it when men call her honey; I'd have spit in his wrinkled face—"you're undercutting your own husband. Listen. Sweetheart. Jack would never sell this for five bucks." He brings the drill so close to her face I flinch.

She blinks hard, sort of coming to, then backs away to get him in focus. "What would he sell it for?"

"Thirteen-fifty. Give or take a couple of bits."

She jerks the drill away from him. "I changed my mind. You can buy this from me for nine ninety-nine. That way . . ." She looks toward the ceiling, eyes moving as if she's watching flocks of birds flying around. She can do that, doesn't matter how many numbers. "That way you make seventeen fifty-one with me. With Jack you'd only make fourteen dollars."

They strike the deal. Nine-fifty apiece for every one of Dad's power tools—thirty-seven including six from the attic above the garage. Three hundred and fifty-one dollars and fifty cents—twenty-five dollars more than Dad paid for the De Soto when it was barely five years old.

Walleye backs his yellow truck up to the garage. "Jack's gonna kill me," he keeps saying, loading as fast as he can.

Mitzy stops next to him, holding a steel fishing spear like the guy on the tuna can. "You pass the dump," she says, barely lisping. "Drop those tires off." She nods toward the wall, and before he can say no, we load eleven threadbare tires into his truck, knowing they'd have been worth a lot in the next worldwide rubber shortage.

Word of our garage sale streaks through downtown Acorn Lake, and people keep coming until Sunday afternoon, when we're down to five stragglers digging through leftovers.

Mitzy and Davey are at the flaming trash barrel in the field across the road, feeding it cardboard boxes and two hundred and fifteen copies of the Dear Sales Employee letter while I sweep the garage floor with the heavy-duty push broom we saved for ourselves. I won't miss that junk. I stopped pawing through Dad's stuff years ago, pretending it was ours. I sweep at the backs of people's feet, pushing them out of here. This is the biggest thing we've ever done. Bigger than getting married, Mom says. It almost feels like spring.

Mom's counting money, chirping so I'll look over and she can stick her tongue out and waggle her head at me. Finally she shouts: "Six hundred ninety-five dollars and sixty-three cents."

I look up.

"Oh! Wait! Seven hundred." Her voice echoes in the empty garage.

I stare at the massive powder-blue-and-white De Soto we already parked facing the garage. It's being eaten alive by rust. Red blotches stretch from the wheel wells to the shredded vinyl roof. The driver's-side door has been wired shut for so long the wire is rusted.

Mom says, "Bet you never thought I could do it. Did you?"

"Sell it."

"What?"

"The car. Sell it."

She looks confused, but only for a second. "The De Soto? Sell my De Soto?"

"Yeah." I look around our clean garage.

"When?"

"Right now. With all that money you can go pick a better one, pay for it and drive it home."

"A hundred dollars?" she asks, standing up. "You think a hundred dollars?"

"Nah. Go for one-fifty."

She stands on her chair, waving at the stragglers. "Excuse me? People? This car's for sale too. This blue-and-white De Soto." Like we have them in every color. She looks brand-new standing up there waving a fistful of money.

People pause, look at the car, and look away fast, embarrassed for us. Except for one—but that's all you need.

"How much?"

"One-fifty."

Mr. Kahout lifts his feed cap to scratch his head and look insulted. He turns to walk away.

I say, "One hundred?"

Without turning around, he says, "Eighty-five bucks."

Mom says, "Cash."

I smile at Natasha.

At eleven p.m. I leap onto the davenport in my flannel night-gown. I say to Mom, Mitzy and Davey, "We need a vote: (A) Tell Dad there's been a burglary. (B) Torch the garage. (C) Wait inside the garage and when the door opens, shout, *We sold your samples, Jack.*"

Mitzy votes to torch the garage. She lives for fires.

Mom jumps up next to me. We hold each other's elbows for balance because the wobbly cushions make our knees pump. She says, "Walleye Watson himself said to me, 'Marion, Jack could take a few lessons from you.' Did you hear him say that? Did you hear it?"

Davey leans his head to the right. "But maybe it really is Dad's money. They were his samples." He thinks about it and leans to the left. "But we did the work."

Mom tells him he's her little diplomat. Then we ignore him.

At midnight I'm lying in bed, picturing Dad sitting in his old Caddy, facing the garage. Randy lifts the overhead door. Empty. He lifts it again. Empty. No De Soto, no samples, no rubber tires or crumpled newspapers, no torn boots or broken sleds or bits of twine because what we couldn't sell we gave away and the rest we burned. We don't need his stuff.

I smell like the garage, but I've never felt so clean. I want more. I want that hall closet empty—grade school projects, overcoats, baby clothes—all flaming in the burn barrel. We'll use the box of Clue and Candyland parts for kindling. Deer season's coming soon, and even though Randy will be gone, Dad will migrate north and we can do the entire house.

Our only mistake was not buying Mom another car. We failed to figure out that once you sell yours, you can't get to a used-car lot to pick out another one. It's like eating your seed corn. Now Dad will grab the three hundred dollars I left on his dresser. He'll shout until Mom falls to her knees, head bowed, offering up the bladeless black ice skate with the four hundred eighty-five dollars I hid in its toe—when it never would have occurred to him that we have the brains to hide the bulk of our profits. Then she'll be car-less for weeks until he brings home one so trashy I'll still have to lie down on the seat going through town. And who knows how long it'll be before Mom rises up again.

I'm drifting off to sleep. I dream the garage door flips open again and Dad's deep inside looking out at me. But I'm Mom. I sit up in bed, tongue as dry as Styrofoam.

Loud honking drags me out of another dream. I don't know what time it is. Mom must have turned on the yard lights. The ceiling is glowing like a TV screen. She and Davey tiptoe into the room Mitzy and I share, and the four of us kneel hip to hip on my bed, looking down out the window, hands templed on the sill like a pew full of sorry Catholics.

Mom whispers, "Thank God he parked in the driveway," and rests her forehead on her hands.

He overshot the driveway. His Cadillac is mostly on the lawn.

I wrap an arm around Mom.

Randy gets out, opens the back door of the car, and Happy bounds out to pee on a rear tire, lifting her leg like a male dog. She'll do it that way for weeks after a hunting trip. Randy's laugh pushes his head back until his mouth is wide open to the stars. He leans forward again to ruffle Happy's fur, both of them thrilled to be alive after riding with Dad behind the wheel. The more Dad drinks, the more he likes driving other people around.

On my left, Davey whispers, "Dad must think the De Soto's in the garage."

Mom doesn't lift her head. "I'd kill myself now and get it over with, but Davey still needs me."

Mitzy's arm comes from the other side to rest beneath mine on Mom's back.

Dad steps out of the car, spinning like bugs are flying in his face.

Davey says, "Maybe he hasn't thought about the De Soto yet."

Dad and Randy are wearing cattail-colored hunting jackets. Randy's yellow hair sticks out of the cap he camouflaged with dry markers. While Dad lights a cigarette, Randy hauls the folded-down canvas tent out of the trunk. Next he takes ducks out and lays them in the driveway, dark heaps against the pink crushed rock.

Dad spots our outlines up in the window and pumps his hands above his head, not knowing he's twenty feet from the emptiest garage in Sioux County. We start to laugh. Needing sleep makes you laugh. So does being scared. We stop, and one of us starts again.

Mitzy says, "Wait a sec," lisping all over the window. "How many ducks have they got there?"

I say, "I've never theen tho many," and start to laugh, but they ignore me.

"Kids, help me keep him out of the garage tonight," Mom says. "We'll all handle this better after a good night's sleep." I doubt she's slept more than a few hours since the garage sale idea struck her, and no one crashes harder than Mom does.

"I'm not afraid of him." Mitzy shakes her fist. "I'll tell him we sold his samples and Lillian sold your car."

"No," Mom says. "Not tonight. We'll figure it all out in the morning."

"We'll still be cleaning ducks in the morning," I say.

· · ·

It's dark outside, except where Randy kneels on the tarp in pools of yellow light coming from the spotlights on the eaves. Dad's standing over him, his finger throwing a stick-like shadow wherever he points. "Twenty-two, twenty-three. Randy, do three rows. No. Christ, are you stupid? Can't you make an arc? Just mallards up top. Twenty-four, twenty-five. Hey, kid. Look at that! We shot twenty-six mallards."

I walk around the tarp. They must have shot everything that moved—mallards, pintails, coots, mergansers, four wood ducks, a pair of loons, a red fox and two chipmunks. Aside from exceeding the legal limits, they broke six Fish and Game rules, starting with no hens, no wood ducks, and most of all, no loons. Shooting the Minnesota State Bird is like stealing mail. That's what Mom would say, and Dad would say, *Only if you get caught.* Then he'd look at her like she's stupid.

Dad's best moods always come right after he's poached something: a pheasant picking gravel on the roadside, a couple of mallards in May or a calf too close to the edge of a farmer's field. Dad keeps his perfectly oiled shotgun in a zippered case in the trunk of his car and his rifles in three racks on the living room wall. He always says taking good care of guns is all he learned from his dad. Then Mom makes bug eyes at us behind his back, meaning he learned everything he knows from his dad—but not how to work hard. His father worked seven days a week.

Dad's standing next to Randy, patting him on the back until he's grinning and bobbing like Wally Cleaver.

Dad says, "Mitzy, doll-face, get the camera for your old dad." And she skips off like he shot her full of eight hours of sleep. The stupid dog follows her.

Mom, Davey and I circle the tarp again, asking how many,

what kind, who shot what. I'm thinking, *Great ducks, Dad, and by the way, we sold the De Soto along with every power tool in your fucking garage.*

When Mom drops to her knees, I'm sure she fell asleep, but she says, "Okey-dokey, folks, let's wrap this baby up for the night," and starts squat-walking, rolling dead game into the tarp like roast turkey into a piece of lefse—shocking Dad right up onto his tiptoes. His head shoots forward.

"What the living hell are you doing?"

"Sweetheart, we're too pooped to pop tonight."

Davey nods once, so tired it nearly topples him.

"You're tired?" Dad pokes himself in the chest. "I've been out in a goddamned swamp all week, freezing my ass off behind a flimsy duck blind, sleeping in a tent. I've been eating out of cans."

Mom says, "Ducks will stay fresh outdoors for as much as twenty-four hours if they're wrapped up tight in a good tarp." She takes another step.

Dad looks confused. When he brings ducks home, we clean ducks. Slowly, he leans down toward her. "Marion?"

"Dad, no," Randy says.

"Marion, are you trying to drive me crazy?" He tilts his head and lowers his face until it's level with hers, so close they might be getting ready to kiss. He shouts, "What the hell is wrong with you?"

"No!" Randy grabs Dad's arm, spins him around, and drags him away from Mom. "Could you stop it? Could you just for one night stop it?" Randy's big hand is holding Dad's sleeve. I'm staring at a ridge of bony knuckles when it comes to me that in all the fights they've had, it only felt like they were using their fists.

They've never touched each other until now. Randy takes his hand back slowly and they step apart. He looks like he might cry. "I got eight lousy days left. Can you give me that much?"

Mom tries to sneak another step, but the movement catches Dad's eye. He looks surprised to see she's still down there. He shakes his head. "Marion," he says finally, "I said *now*. Right now." And he sets his booted foot down on the tarp in front of her. No one moves. A long time goes by before I realize we're waiting for Randy, but he's inching away from us, rubbing one hand with the other, just watching.

Mom lifts a foot to try another step. Dad sets his boot sole against her shoulder and pushes, rolling her over like an egg. While Randy and I are shouting, "Dad, Dad, Dad," Davey drops down next to her, automatically. She's lying on her side with her back against the black-and-white loons, knees tucked up, hands together under her cheek as if she'd just as soon we all tiptoed off and let her sleep. I picture Randy, Mitzy, me and Davey, lying at her feet in birth order, a row of nested commas. I should have fallen automatically.

Randy grabs Dad's shoulders, pulls him close, then shoves him hard. "How do you like it?" Dad catches his balance, lunges forward and pushes Randy in the chest with both hands. But Randy stays as still as a steel beam. A second later, he steps sideways to draw Dad away from Mom. I look down. Her eyes are squeezed shut as if the lights hurt. From the corner of my eye, I see Randy swing around with his fist coming down full force at Dad—and I'm in between them, screaming, "Randy. Don't. Don't." I'm pushing him back while Dad tries to shove me aside to get to him. Mom and Davey are on their feet. Their small fingers pull at our cheeks and necks, trying to separate us. We push and shove, grunting, crying out, until the energy disappears like the last bit of water getting sucked down the drain. We step apart, shocked, not believing that could have been us fighting like a bunch of poor people. Mom wraps her arms around Davey and rests her chin on his head.

We're still standing around like strangers waiting for a bus when Mitzy sprints out of the dark. "What's going on?" Happy circles us, licking fingers and nuzzling thighs. When no one answers, Mitzy raises the camera and we step into position.

Our photograph albums are page after page of people posing with dead animals: the four of us touching a row of gutted deer hanging from the oak tree; Randy holding up a twenty-pound Canadian honker; Randy holding a string of snowshoe rabbits; Dad pointing at a pair of bucks strapped upside down to his car. You won't get your picture taken at our house without a dead animal.

First Mitzy and I sit next to the ducks. Then Randy and Davey. Finally, Randy takes one of Mom and Dad. Mom's kneeling, staring out beyond Randy, glassy-eyed, while Dad stands behind her, glaring into the lens.

By three a.m. we look like a poultry-packing night shift crew. At just this point of every duck season, it hits me that the more ducks they shoot the more we have to eat, months of birds tough as beef jerky, biting down on buckshot like a hatchet ripping through your fillings into the roots of your teeth. But when they first wake us with a car full of fresh game, we slip right out of our dreams and into theirs, whooping it up like starving prairie settlers instead of six people living five miles from a town with its own damned grocery store.

Mom sits slumped on a wooden chair where the narrow kitchen opens onto the square living and dining area. Her legs are spread wide and she's holding a mallard hen upside down by its feet with its head in a paper bag on the floor while she tears off its feathers. In back of her, at the dining room table, Davey's kneeling on a chair, wearing blue jeans and a cowboy pajama top, butcher knife raised above the wood carving board, ready to chop off legs and wing tips. "Careful, honey," Mom says every time she hands him a duck, and he says, "Okay, Mom," then brings the knife down so hard we flinch. When he's done with a few, he brings them to me at the stove.

Behind me the refrigerator opens for the third time, making that sucking sound like it wants to stay closed. The milk bottle slides across the tinny metal shelf. Ice cubes hit the glass. Dad burps. He's drinking fast tonight, mixing his scotch and milk as loud as a dare.

If you ever have to pluck ducks, ask to be the dipper. That's my job. You grab a duck by its neck, dip it into a twelve-quart stockpot full of hot water and melted paraffin wax, count one, two, three, lift it high, swivel right, and dip the newly waxed duck into a sink of ice water. Dip, swivel, dip. Hot, swivel, cold. I'm in a three a.m. duck-dipping trance, jolted awake every third or fourth duck by the vision of the garage door flipping open and nothing being in there except the push broom. I'm smiling into the stockpot, too tired to be scared. Dad rattles his ice cubes, and my head feels like a Yahtzee cup.

I set a waxed wood duck in the cold-water sink and drape its head over the edge so Mitzy has something to grip. I'm ahead of her. There's a five-duck backup in the water.

Dad takes a noisy breath and lets it out in stages.

Still wearing her baby-doll pajama top, Mitzy pins a merganser to the counter with the heel of one hand, wedges the fingers of the other under the hardened wax, screws her lips up and pulls so fast there's a tearing noise as the pinfeathers are ripped out. She loves that part so much that sometimes you can hear a little grunt from the back of her throat. I think she waits all year for this.

Dad's boots squeak on the tile as he turns to Davey. "C'mon. Pay attention here. Just the wing tips. There's good meat in the wings."

The butcher knife whacks the cutting board.

"Careful, honey."

Dad rattles his glass.

Mitzy strips the wax off a coot. Most people won't eat coots, but Dad says if it was good enough for the Indians, it's good enough for the Andersons.

I want to tell him we should start saving duck feet. They might be worth a lot someday, and we've got room to store them now. The garage door flips open: no power tools or sets of Melmac dishes. Mitzy will tell him I sold the De Soto because whatever pops into Mitzy's head pops right back out her mouth. Mom claims Dad ignores me because of my sharp tongue. But it's because he knows whose side I'm on.

Maybe I'll play dead.

He's standing where he can watch Randy.

I'll pretend I'm paralyzed. I'll slide to the floor.

Randy always has the worst part. He takes an ice-cold dripping-wet featherless duck from Mitzy, lays it out all beige and puckered on the pullout breadboard, slices it from belly to chest and guts it. Tonight as always though, he does it perfectly, so Dad turns toward Mom and burps in three descending notes, mouth open, good as a *fuck you* because burping's on the list of things she thinks people should go into the bathroom to do. She ignores it, but it's too late for being careful. He's winding up. He turns back to Randy. "Jesus Christ. Where the hell did you learn to gut a duck?" His words are getting slurry.

Mom cleaned all the game herself until Randy got old enough to learn. Now he slices into a large gizzard, cuts away the sandy part and sets the good pieces on a sheet of freezer paper with the other giblets. His long fingers fold the ends of the paper around the pile, roll it twice and tape it shut with a three-inch piece of masking tape.

"Look," Dad says, "you're throwing away half the gizzard."

"No," Randy says, dragging out the *o*, his voice tight as wire. He writes GIBLETS on the packet in his perfect block letters with the black laundry marker.

The kitchen windows are propped open to cut the gamy smell, and the freezing wind off the lake is hitting my neck. I lean forward, sink my arms into the hot water, and shiver like a girl who's being electrocuted.

Behind me there's a hard-edged *click* as Dad flips open his Zippo. Then a metal scrape and a *puff-puff-puff* as he lights another cigarette. Then a quiet space. Then the freezer opens, ice cubes hit the glass, boots squeak and, as if he's been holding it in for his entire life, Dad says, "Jesus fucking Christ, Randy! Do you get it? Do you understand where you're headed?"

I pull my arms out of the water, spin around, and by the time I've backed up against the stove, Randy is facing Dad, and Mom is on her feet. "Leave him alone," she says. "Right now, Jack. Leave him alone."

With his fingertip touching Randy's jaw like the end of a

pistol, Dad looks at Mom. "Your son here acts like nothing's up. This whole fucking family acts like nothing's up. How can that be?"

"How can you act like he has a choice? We don't have a choice in this."

Randy's face is blank. His yellow hair is hanging out the back of his cap and over his collar. Mitzy's leaning against the sink, cradling a wet duck. Davey's still at his chair, looking the same as always except for the water running down his face.

"Am I alone here?" Dad says. "Tell me. Am I the only one in this household who's not lost in some kind of fucking fantasyland?" He looks around at Mom, Mitzy, Davey and me, drunk enough to be dangerous but a long way from passing out. It's the worst time. "Well, I've got news from the real world: This stupid kid here is going to get a free haircut from the United States Army and then he's going to go get himself killed in Vietnam. They're going to steal Jack Anderson's son and they're going to send him back home in a body bag."

Mom's on him, beating on his shoulders, pushing him like a snowplow. He looks surprised as he stumbles, but it's like falling in a crowded school bus, and he catches himself on the counter, scotch and milk slopping out of the highball glass, running off his wrist. He sets the glass down, and by the time he straightens up, his face is hard again. He dives at her, but Randy's there. Randy digs his fingers into the front of Dad's shirt, lifts him out of the kitchen, drives him backward into the living room, hesitates for a heartbeat and punches him—a quick punch to the jaw, a pulled punch, but it sets Dad on his ass. Randy leans down, lifts him up, lets him fall and punches him again while he's still in the air. Blood shoots from his nose as he hits the floor, and I hear us crying.

Randy has him again, like a sandbag, one hand in his collar, one in his belt, when Mom grabs Randy's arm. She looks in through his eyes, and as she shakes her head, her open hand inches up to the side of his neck and starts to stroke him. I'd forgotten the way she always settled him down when we were little, like he was a wild horse she'd found in the field. "Shhhhh," she says. "Randy. Randy, just think about something pleasant." He doesn't move. It seems as if he's waiting for information to come out of the palm of her hand and in through his skin. "Shhhh," she says again. Slowly, he lets go of Dad and backs away, raising his hands. He turns to walk toward the door, long-legged, narrow-waisted, with his hands still in the air and his wool shirt pulling between his wide shoulders at every step.

The front door shuts with a soft click, and as the storm door wheezes shut I look down at Dad, sitting on the sticky floor, legs out front, hands cupped over his nose to catch the blood. I dip a dishrag in the cold-water sink, wring it out and hand it down to him.

"Thanks."

I step away.

Mom helps him up.

I stand next to Mitzy and Davey. We're facing Mom and Dad across the narrow kitchen with nowhere else to look, inhaling the stink of wild game, wet wool and cigarettes until I feel mildewed as the canvas tent.

Dad takes the dishrag away from his face. "I can't believe they can just take your son." A drop of blood rolls out of his nose and down his upper lip. It disappears into his mouth. He tilts his head back, squeezes the bridge of his nose between two fingers and refolds the dishrag against his thigh. "Jesus, Marion," he says quietly. His face is puckered as if he's going to cry, but it passes fast. He says, "I'm a real prick sometimes, aren't I?"

Mom sets her hand on his waist as if saying you're a prick proves you can't be one. He lays an arm across her shoulders, but as she leans into him with a sigh, he pulls away. He starts patting all his pockets, front and back, hunting for the Zippo he's had since World War II, a lighter so lucky it never saw action. He shines it on his sleeve—one side, then the other, tiny arcs of blood trapped in his cuticles. "I'm going to give him this."

Mom nods.

He looks at it more closely, flips it open, lights it, shuts it, does it one more time—and drops it back into his shirt pocket. "That kid would lose a good lighter like this in a week. But I've got something for him." When he heads for the door, no one else moves. "Come on. The kid's out there hiding in the damned garage. I'm going to give him that switchblade he always wanted."

Outside, we follow him in single file along the stepping-stone path, through the spotlights, all of us walking toward it now, with me at the tail end, hanging back. I picture us making a run for it, splitting up so he won't know who to go after. In front of me, Davey's arms have gone limp, and in front of him, Mitzy's hugging herself, freezing in the little jacket she threw on over her pajamas. Mom's up there right behind Dad. I remind myself the garage sale was her idea, then I remember the De Soto.

At the side door to the garage, Dad pauses and turns toward us with his face so lit up you'd think giving away a knife would stop a war. As if this will fix everything. Ollie-ollie-oxen-free. But Randy stopped wanting that switchblade years ago.

The door behind Dad is ajar, framing him in gold from the overhead light in the garage. He's only a little drunk now, and with his blue eyes and blond crew cut he might be a handsome version of a regular father. He leans out to the side as if he's going to count to make sure we're all here. He looks past Mom and Mitzy and Davey, and he smiles at me. Looks right into my eyes and smiles. And I'm so surprised it's as if I fell out of a tree. It's a warm smile, an entire-face smile, as if he's happy to look at me. I don't understand. But someone should punch the bastard every morning.

When he turns to open the door, I step out of line. I reach toward him. "Wait," I say. I'm ready to apologize. I'm about to say, *Dad! Hold on a second, will you?* But Mom turns toward me and I see her face. My mother believes it finally happened. She thinks the one thing big enough to make him realize how much he loves us finally happened and she already sold our chance at a garage sale.

Dad opens the door and as he steps into the light, it settles on me like a sick joke that if it weren't the empty garage it would be something else. I know it. Tonight or tomorrow he'd go back to being himself. It would be over something big or small, but it would be automatic. It would be his chocolate-covered peanuts or his clean socks or his shotgun shells or his wife—something he thinks we stole from him. I know it, in the same way I know I saw him love me for a few seconds just now. It was in his eyes, it was everywhere in his face, and it was something.

Salad Girls

*F*riday night we're running through the hidden halls under the Minneapolis/St. Paul International Airport, six pairs of loafers slapping cement as we bump into each other, jerking arms out of jackets, unwrapping scarves, panting like bird dogs by the time we reach the last corner. I toss a mitten away with a cigarette, stoop to snag its thumb, and look up to see Melody, our three-hundred-pound night-shift manager, waiting by the gray steel time clock, bellowing like a bull.

"It's twenty-seven minutes *after* midnight." She's taller than the Foshay Tower. "Six Acorn Lake salad girls times twenty-seven minutes late. Two hours and forty-two minutes behind schedule with a seven-twenty-seven sitting on the runway blowing fuel at a hundred bucks a minute waiting for two hundred hard-boiled-egg-and-black-olive salads, thirty-two first-class shrimp cocktail cups, and four hundred moist towelettes. You girls don't want these jobs, there's more girls right behind you. Lots more girls."

With a hiccup and a moan, Prissy starts to weep. We've been taking care of her since her mother's big Catholic funeral eight weeks ago. Breast cancer. Thirty-seven. So young even the Lutherans came to the wake for a beer and soft good-bye.

"Prissy's fine," I say.

Melody's been willing to ignore the fact that except for Prissy, we're all fifteen. We're under age. We've hung on to these jobs for three months even though we've been late every night since Prissy's mom died, but Melody knows all she has to do is fire Prissy and we're all fired. We'll be girls without a ride.

"Prissy's cool." I punch her card and slip it into the metal wall rack. Driving sixty-two miles each way to the airport Friday and Saturday nights is wearing her down, but the night shift pays a dollar seventy-three an hour. Our only other hope for work is washing sheets and dumping bedpans at the Credit River Retirement Farm for a buck an hour, and we've already done that.

"Prissy's just an emotional girl." Irene steers her away with an arm around her shoulders, laying a trail of Tabu eau de cologne. "Come on, honey."

We didn't know mothers could die. No one mentions it.

The twins, Tina and Sherry, are both trying to stick their cards into the time clock. Tiny, blond and perfectly matched, they pull their cards away and say in unison, "No, you go," then reach back in together, then pull away. "No, you go."

"Why do I have to pay for two of you?" Melody holds up two fingers to clarify.

Natasha looks down at the twins, her dark eyes bulging as she grabs both cards in one wide hand and punches them in. *Chunk-chunk.* Farm girls do everything fast—except the twins, who get distracted, circling one another like they're watching themselves on TV, too confused to concentrate on anything.

I punch in and hurry to catch up with the other girls, but behind me Melody laughs—more like a short bark—and I force myself to slow down to a stroll. As my steps echo off the tile floor and the bare white walls and my breathing goes ragged, she laughs again.

In the ladies' changing room, we toss our clothes into clanging metal lockers and grab white uniforms that have been starched and pressed, folded flat and pressed again, sealed shut thin as record albums. We shake them open like grocery bags and pull them on over bras and panties. The stiff A-line dresses come only in Melody's size, making the girls in front of me look like a row of Christmas bells racing toward the industrial kitchen. I always slow down where the warm bakery smells of cinnamon, butter and sugar are tangled up with the icy jet exhaust billowing in through the loading dock.

At our three a.m. break, we sit slumped under the cold fluorescent lights in the employee cafeteria, facing each other across a table, looking like somebody's collection of hunchbacked girls. Except Irene. On my left, she's sitting up straight even though she's the tallest girl in school, not counting her sisters. She looks like her mother, a blonde with slitty Japanese-looking eyes. It stops people. Now Irene's staring up at the mirror in her Cover Girl compact, mouth open wide as she applies another layer of mascara, so absorbed you'd never guess she just peeled and deveined two hundred and twelve half-frozen shrimp. Her regulation black hair net sits perfectly on her bleached French twist. Even at three a.m. Irene looks great, but we don't mind because she's always cutting bangs for one of us, trimming split ends for another. She likes to rat up my hair. *Lillian,* she'll say, *your face is so narrow that even with bone-straight hair you need to go wide on the sides. Real wide sides.*

We pass around a pack of Salems. Across from me Prissy sits between the twins, small round eyes staring straight through the table while she blots blood from her fingertips with a napkin. Tina takes a deep pull off her cigarette and holds the smoke in while she leans over and slides the cigarette between Prissy's wire-thin lips. *Inhale,* we all say, like the amen at the end of a long prayer.

I unwind a warm sweet roll, tilt my head back and feed myself a spongy dough strip, then follow it with a long drag off a cigarette, wash it down with Pepsi and start all over again. If I could smoke through my ears while I eat through my mouth, I'd do it that way instead. Mom's the same, but the sweet rolls never go to her hips. After four kids, she's still thin. Worn out, but thin.

On my right, Natasha stops eating the apple she brought from home and waves my smoke away with one big hand, making *pfft pfft pfft* noises as if I'm poisoning her air. Our fight started the first day of first grade. We agree on exactly nothing.

The six of us are alone in the cafeteria except for two old bakers sitting a few tables away. On their way out, the one I've never seen before does a double take and stops to look hard at Natasha. "Holy Christ, you gotta be a Kahout. One of Earl Kahout's kids, right?"

Natasha's head drops like a basketball into her crossed arms. She groans.

"Am I right or am I right? Sioux County?" His face has a buttery shine.

"Fuck off," she mutters into her elbows.

I've never heard Natasha say *fuck.* It wakes me up. She never does anything bad. She's not human. On Halloween night after even the twins had finally gone all the way with their boyfriends, Irene renamed Natasha *Our Virgin of the Lake.*

"Which number are you?" the baker asks.

She won't answer.

"Natasha's number ten," I volunteer, then elbow her to make sure she's not missing out on this.

The baker smirks like everyone does when they're counting Kahouts. The kids are easy marks, every one of them with their mother's dark, bulging eyes. "Your friend the youngest?" he asks me.

Natasha's mother is seven months pregnant with number fourteen. Her father's waiting to climb the steel rungs on the out-side of the silo with a bucket of red paint so he can change the five-foot-tall number *thirteen* to *fourteen,* like a man keeping score at a baseball game.

Thank God my dad doesn't like babies. They're no different than cigarettes. You try one because your friends are doing it, and then can't remember why you should stop. The real trick is not having the first one.

The baker looks back and forth from Natasha to his buddy, bouncing around like some fool on a game show, dirty brown hair sticking out the bottom of the paper chef's hat he's wearing like a prize. Suddenly I like him even less than I like Natasha.

"Good night," I say.

"Wait."

"Fuck off." I turn away.

Across the table, Prissy's trying to suck the dried napkin off her fingertips. She was the smartest girl in our grade until her mother died, and I'm starting to wonder whether she'll ever be smart again. Maybe if something bad enough happens when you're young, you never get your real self back. But Prissy doesn't seem to remember she used to be some other way. She's concentrating on spitting out bits of paper napkin stuck to her tongue like tobacco from an unfiltered Camel.

"No more eggs tonight," Irene tells her. Prissy spent the first three hours of the shift perched on a tall stool at the two-foot-deep stainless-steel sink, peeling hard-boiled eggs under the running tap, the only job she's wanted to do since her mom died. She likes the water running up her wrists, across the soft skin on the insides of her arms, all the way to her elbows. We all do, but the water softens up your fingers until the eggshells rip through them like razor blades, and because your hands are numb, you don't realize how badly you've been hurt until much later.

"I always rinse the blood off the eggs," Prissy says, her face a pale oval. "Nobody but us ever sees it."

She hasn't said that much at one time since the funeral. Irene and I raise our eyebrows at each other, sharing hope.

Natasha's head is still down. I elbow her again. "You peel for the rest of the night. Prissy can slice."

"You're not my mother."

I rest my hand on her shoulder, lean close, and whisper in her ear, "And for that I'm grateful."

Irene laughs and licks the dull tip of her stubby eyebrow pencil.

"Natasha," I say, "you ought to talk to your mother about birth control. Open up by telling her how many eggs you sliced tonight. Then slip right on into the issue of sperm."

Irene pounds the table and whoops once real loud. The twins look at each other, each one hoping the other got it.

Prissy sounds like she's talking in her sleep. "I wish my mom had had fourteen kids instead of just me."

"No, you don't," Natasha says into her arms.

"Oh, but I do. You see, if your mom dies, say she dies giving birth—it happens, you know—well, if your mother dies, at least there will be other people left."

Natasha looks up. "Don't be dense. Women don't die in childbirth anymore. We're not living on the fucking buffalo prairies here."

"Back off," I say, looking at her more closely.

"We had an aunt who died having a baby," Sherry says. She and Tina hook eyes over Prissy's bent head and say, "Bled to death."

"At least the baby lived," Tina says, nodding at Sherry. "So it wasn't a total loss." She thinks about it. Sherry speaks for her. "Sort of one for one . . . so really the father came out even. It was a girl. You see, it was like he traded the mother for the daughter."

"Except that he couldn't get more kids," Tina says.

"Because he didn't have a wife," Sherry says.

"I think we get it," I say.

"But he found a new wife."

Natasha's eyes bulge out farther. "Who cares about your aunt? She probably had the kid in the barn."

Prissy's head rolls around on her shoulders twice as if she's coming unscrewed at the neck. "My mom died and my dad still has me, but . . ." She stops to examine a slice on the tip of her baby finger.

"Honey, you look just like her," Irene says, rubbing pink lipstick off her top teeth with her finger. "If you'd go a little darker blond, maybe use brown eyeliner like she did. Your mom sure used a lot of brown, right there in the corners."

Prissy looks lost. "He still misses her."

"You get to keep her clothes, don't you?" Irene asks. She's been wondering for weeks.

"That's it," I whisper to her. "Buy the man a few more shots of Jack Daniel's, dress his daughter up like his dead wife, steer her into Bud's Bowling and Brew, and watch him go all the way around the bend. We'll do it right after work."

Natasha interrupts. "In the United States of America, women don't die giving birth anymore."

"But our aunt . . . ." says Sherry.

"Who cares? Your uncle probably called the vet when her water broke. My mom had thirteen. Hell, Irene's mom had almost that many. Not a hitch. Wham-bam. Couple of sharp pains and they're out."

"You're so lucky," Prissy says.

"God *designed* women to have babies."

"If your mom died . . ."

"Will you wake up? She's pregnant, not malignant."

Prissy starts to cry.

"I'm sorry," Natasha says, reaching for her hand. "Prissy, I'm really sorry."

"Girls!" Melody fills the cafeteria doorway like a new refrigerator. "Wake up and smell the airport. We need a hundred and eight cream-cheese and-olive sandwiches on the blue Braniff plates. You are not at the prom."

I like Melody. She makes a big deal out of everything.

"There's always another jet sitting on the runway waiting for food. Get used to it, girls, or get out of the business while you're young."

. . .

By five a.m. we've been up almost twenty-four hours. Food falls from our hands. We stare as radishes and green olives roll down our slanted worktables, past elbows, off toward the floor below. We take baby steps through slimy layers of wet lettuce and cherry tomatoes, broken eggs and Swiss cheese, hugging five-pound cans of black olives and bucket-sized metal bowls of iceberg lettuce, shuffling back and forth from the walk-in coolers to the giant stainless-steel tables.

Everything in the kitchen is oversized and heavy, as if they planned on hiring much larger people. No one has the energy for more than a word, even though we know Melody's sleeping in her office with the door locked, half-hour inspections over for the night. The only way you get through the final hours of the night shift is a minute at a time. Thinking about your paycheck no longer helps, although it'll matter like crazy later. You need to break the minutes down into bits of food. Sometimes counting helps: one olive, two olives, three olives.

I stand at a table in the center of the room, breaking pieces off a sour-smelling block of blue cheese the size of a tree stump. Strands of hair escape my hair net, drawn toward the moldy bits of cheese I leave on my face every time I scratch an itch. I rub my eye against the clean shoulder of my uniform, leaving a smudge of yesterday's mascara. In school Monday, my hair will smell like a pack of wet retrievers even though I'll have rinsed it in vinegar time and time again. But we all skip a lot of school. Mostly Mondays. But lots of Tuesdays. Some Fridays. Except Natasha.

She's at the sink, peeling eggs. Next to her, Prissy slices. Down the way, the twins stand on wooden milk crates, arranging Boston lettuce leaves on a sea of powder-blue Braniff plates, moving as if they're underwater. Across from me Irene's lining up tiny paper cups on a cookie sheet three feet long, then filling them with cream from a two-gallon pitcher. By five-thirty she's stopped lifting the spout after each cup, and just runs a slow line of cream up and down the rows.

At six-thirty, Loading Dock Tim slips into the kitchen to stand next to Irene in his dark green jumpsuit. He spends his breaks studying her as if she's casting spells. Now he watches while she caps the floating cups, then lifts one side of the cookie sheet a few inches and pours the extra cream toward a floor drain clogged with a parsley forest. She smiles up at him, and shyly he holds out one of the miniature liquor bottles he finds on the dirty trays. She tucks it into a patch pocket on the front of her uniform. He hands her another, then another and another as if he's delivering gems to the Queen of Sheba, all the while swaying around on feet that seem nailed to the floor. I wonder how much he had to drink to get the guts to approach her.

When Irene's pockets are full, she lobs a bottle of Beefeater's into my cheese. I lick it off, unscrew the cap and empty it in one gulp, like chugging pine-scented polish remover. My tongue burns. My throat bursts into flames. I've never liked booze, but now I wait, hoping something will change. Anything.

"Smart," says Natasha. She swiveled her stool around and is leaning back on her elbows against the edge of the sink, her long legs dangling, feet just missing the floor. All the Kahouts are tall. "Real smart," she says. "Like you're still in first grade."

"Up yours."

Tim throws a little bottle at her with more energy than I thought he owned. But she catches it with a quick forearm lift, leans forward and fires it past me so close I have to jump backward.

"Inside!" Tim says.

Irene's laughing, a tinkling laugh like a xylophone. She salutes me with a bottle of vodka, and drinks it down, laughing so hard she snorts. I love it that she snorted. She wipes vodka from the tip of her nose with the back of her hand, then pulls out a small tray and sets it up with six paper drinking cups, which she fills with gin and brandy and sherry, mixing two kinds of liquor if she runs out mid-cup.

Tim eases the tray up onto his shoulder as if he's been a waiter all his life. He sways through the garbage soup on the floor to where the twins stand on their milk crates. He presents it to them on bended knee like they're city girls with diamond studs in their ears.

Tina and Sherry each pick a cup and take a sip.

"Toss it back," Tim says. He demonstrates without so much as wiggling the tray. "Hair of the dog," he says and burps.

The twins look at each other, then toss it back. As they cough and sputter, Irene glides toward them, nodding steadily as she tears small pieces off a loaf of Braniff first-class French bread tucked under her arm. She feeds a piece to each of them.

Prissy walks over and drinks from a cup, slips off her hair net, shakes her hair free and kneels. Tenting her small hands, she lifts her bare face and sticks out her narrow pink tongue. Irene sets a piece of the torn bread on it, cups Prissy's chin in her hand and holds it.

"Ominous dominoes," Irene says in a deep voice. She dips two fingers into one of the cups and makes the sign of the cross over Prissy's upturned face.

Tears run from Prissy's eyes. She sobs once and bows her head.

I take a sip of something terrible, kneel beside Prissy in the cool wet lettuce leaves and stick out my tongue.

"*You're* not Catholic!" Natasha says. "You can't do that." She pauses, looks surprised for a second, then starts in again, jabbing her finger toward us. "You're all going straight to hell." She pauses again, then spins away from us. As she grips the edge of the sink, her whole body jerks forward and she throws up all over the wall behind the egg-peeling sink.

I'm sitting on a bed of wet lettuce, laughing, when Natasha stops long enough to turn and scowl at me. "Fuck you, Lillian."

I clap my hands above my head and whistle.

She starts to cry. The only thing I ever liked about her is that she's not a crier, but she's sobbing full-out when the heaving starts again, spraying the off-white wall with bits of red apple peel.

Tim looks embarrassed and turns away, as if throwing up belongs in the ladies' room like the white metal machines full of disposable sanitary napkins.

Irene dips her fingers in a cup of liquor and shakes her hand toward Natasha. "Vomitus dominoes." She dips her fingers again and sprinkles the twins.

I should have been more alert. If I hadn't let my guard down, I'd have heard Melody coming down the hall. But it would have been too late anyway, much too late, and shoulda-woulda-coulda buys nothing. She stands near the door, gripping the side of a stainless-steel shelving unit piled to the ceiling with plastic plates and bowls, all of it shaking and rattling while her mouth opens and closes as if the sound's turned off. Her face looks soft and fat without her fierce red lipstick. It hits me that she was pretty once.

Melody doesn't have to tell us we're fired. We help each other up and stagger out of the kitchen, exhausted all over again, giggling, a little drunk and still a little scared of Melody. We're halfway down the hall before she gets her voice back. "You have to clean this up. I *won't* clean this. They can't pay me enough . . ." Tim pushes the giant loading dock doors closed behind us with a rubbery *whoosh*.

I'm surprised to see the tarmac covered with snow and the wind blowing drifts through the yellow cones from the runway lights. We're standing shoulder to shoulder in the cold when Natasha snaps over double and starts heaving again. Maybe it's the oily jet exhaust blowing in our faces. We jump back, holding our cigarettes clear. Except for Prissy. She hands me hers and goes over to hold back the long black hair that's slipping out of Natasha's hair net.

"Oh, Christ," I say, trying not to retch. "You don't have to do that. Natasha can take care of herself."

Prissy sets a hand on Natasha's high forehead. "Is it the flu?"

Natasha leans down onto Prissy, sweat dripping off her face. She shakes her head.

"You don't feel warm," says Prissy.

"I'm pregnant."

I'm not sure I heard it. "You mean your mother's pregnant." Getting pregnant is the fear that keeps you up all night, leaves you staring out the window in class, making deals with God, swearing you'll never do that again.

"No," Natasha says.

"She's pregnant with her mother," Tina says. Sherry nods.

"Natasha *is* her damned mother," I say.

"That's so cool." Prissy pats Natasha's back. "I'd like to be pregnant."

Irene and I look at each other. Acorn Lake girls who get pregnant visit distant aunts and never come back. Every class has always lost a girl or two. The Class of '63 lost four. We've heard stories about abortions somewhere behind the packing plants in South St. Paul, but they're just rumors and the point is always that the girl died from the rust on the hanger. You'd think they'd learn to bring their own.

"Are you and Billy going to get married?" Prissy asks.

Billy's the principal's son, honor student, football star. They're not even from Acorn Lake, and you can be sure his family has plans for him, better plans than Natasha Kahout.

After changing clothes back in the locker room, we ride the elevator up to the main floor of the airport. The doors slide open, and we back farther into the elevator, squinting, holding our hands up to block the light coming through the floor-to-ceiling windows. When the sun comes up on fresh snow in Minnesota, the snowdrifts and the sky reflect each other until you can't tell up from down because everything is a blinding bluish-white; and when the first snowfall comes just two weeks before Christmas, the magic surprise of it makes you feel like the tiny people in those snow-filled glass domes.

We step onto the marble floor in the vaulted lobby, looking around, blinking like groundhogs. "Chestnuts Roasting on an Open Fire" is oozing out of the overhead sound system, and the smell of a twenty-foot Norwegian pine sweeps over us. It's covered in shiny red balls the size of muskmelons. Three women pass us by, smiling with perfect teeth, all dressed up to fly somewhere, high heels *tickety-tickety* on the shiny floor. Behind them a skycap's pushing a cart of their matched sets of fancy Samsonite luggage. Santa hurries by with a Dalmatian puppy in his arms. A man's voice comes from everywhere at once, announcing a final boarding call for a flight to Paris. It's leaving in ten minutes from the Green Concourse.

"Wake up and smell the airport." Irene stretches her arms above her head, then bends over and presses her nose against her kneecaps to get the kinks out. Her cordovan penny loafers are speckled with coleslaw, but her fingernails are still red. I don't know how she does it.

Natasha pushes on the ends of her long fingers, as if she can reseal the cuts. She tied her hair back with a rubber band, and her face sticks out, square and gray.

I wonder whether people passing us know who smells like vomit and who smells like blue cheese or whether it even matters. Maybe we all smell—just one big stink coming up from the basement.

"Girls." Natasha looks up. "I have great news."

I hope she lied about being pregnant.

"All these goddamned people have to eat our food."

Irene laughs, more of a snort than a laugh because her head's still upside down, like she's kissing her own kneecaps. She opens back up like a jackknife, raises her elbows and pushes up on the hem of her hairdo with the palms of her hands, looking like she's been away on vacation. "What would you do if you were on a plane and you saw blood in your salad?" She crosses her eyes at me.

"Ask me after I've ridden on a plane."

Next to me Natasha stiffens and closes her eyes as if she's going to be sick again, but it passes. I can feel her letting go. We've been fighting for so long I'm an expert on Natasha Amelia Kahout.

We walk off together through the airport, struggling into jackets, pushing out the long wool scarves we threaded through the sleeves.

Just inside the glass doors, we're standing on the rubber mat, wrapping scarves around our necks and faces, turning ourselves into mummies for the long walk to Prissy's mother's car, when three girls appear out of the blurry wall of blowing snow. They can't be more than twenty years old. Big girls, mouth-breathers with doughy-looking faces, they walk into the building and disappear down the hall. I realize I'm leaning after them, staring. I turn, put my shoulder into the door, and fight the wind to open it.

Outside alone, I'm standing in a snowy curtain blowing left to right so thick I can't see beyond the round-shouldered shapes of the buried cars in the front row. And as if it's being piped into my earmuffs, I hear Melody's gravelly voice. "Lots more girls coming right behind you." She laughs. "Salad girls."

There's no path in the snow yet because every footprint gets drifted over before the next one is made. I inch forward, feeling for the hard edge of the high curb through the soles of my loafers, with Melody's voice in my ears making a big deal out of everything.

Less than three weeks later Natasha Amelia Kahout disappears. It's the first day of school she's missed since first grade, so by ten a.m., I'm certain. But I track down the bug-eyed Kahout kids anyway, one after another, just to hear them say they can't remember the name of the town where their sick aunt lives.

On February 6 Mrs. Kahout gives birth to a nine-pound

twelve-ounce baby girl, and I start checking the silo every day when I drive by. February. March. April. The count stays at thirteen, as if Mr. Kahout thinks he came out even. Sort of one for one, as the twins would say.

The twins don't change.

In May, Prissy's still glancing out classroom windows, peeking through doorways. She's started wearing her mother's Monet jewelry and lots of brown eyeliner. Her IQ is still down around her ankles.

Yesterday Irene showed up with hair even redder than mine. She used her mother's dye but left it on for two days instead of twenty minutes so the color would be intense. There's a rumor they'll expel her this afternoon to protect the rest of us.

I'm still inching forward, sometimes hearing Melody's voice, sometimes my mother's, but more often lately it's the *tickety-tickety* of high heels heading for the Green Concourse.

1968

Voluntary Breathers

*M*om's disappointing '59 Ford Fairlane is parked in one side of our horseshoe driveway when Irene and I pull up, its trunk wired shut, hubcaps missing, backseat jammed to the ceiling with overflowing plastic laundry baskets. She should be at the Laundro-Matic; she's been talking about it for weeks. I grew out of clothes trapped in her laundry system until I started doing my wash by hand. That's how you learn, I learned to keep a clean bath towel in my bedroom, too, in a box on the closet floor along with aspirin, tampons, cold pills, and a small supply of canned foods.

But Mom has her good points, like realizing early that I can run my own life. And Dad doesn't care, so I'm blessed with more freedom than anyone I know. I wear what I want, say what I want, come and go as I please. I'm skipping school today with Irene just because it smells like spring.

I ease past a white Firebird parked on the dirt road that snakes around Acorn Lake, and back into the other side of our driveway. "Probably Jehovah's Witnesses selling Watchtower pamphlets," I say. In Acorn Lake you're baptized Lutheran or Catholic and buried the same way. You don't swap sides in the middle, but the hopeful Jehovahs show up twice a year to check the cabins for city people.

As I open the screen door to the house, a strip of dried green paint lets go of the trim and flutters to the cement step. I try to twist the doorknob. "Something's wrong." We never use the lock. I pound. Somewhere inside the house Happy howls. Irene and I run around to the door that faces the lake. The gold drapes are drawn. My sweaty hand slips on the metal knob.

"What kind of mood was she in this morning?" Irene asks as she noses the window screen, one hand above her eyes, long sheets of peroxided hair swinging forward. "You don't think she'd really do it, do you? They say you can ignore the ones who threaten all the time."

I've got a twenty-pound cement block on the backswing, ready to heave it through the picture window when Mom opens the door wearing Dad's old bathrobe, holding the neck closed like she's gone suddenly modest after a lifetime of bikinis and halter tops. She looks like hell—blond curls sticking up, face pale and kind of mashed-in looking, mascara on her cheek.

"What did you take?" I ask, arms trembling as I set the block down and edge closer, afraid of startling her into slamming the door and locking me out again. I picture myself wrestling her to the ground, sticking my fingers down her throat, rescuing her because Irene is wrong; you do have to watch the ones who threaten. They've told you what's on their minds. Mom tells me everything. We're close.

"Hello, Irene!" Mom says as if she's greeting some lady from town who popped in for coffee. Her bright-green eyes are glassy.

I block the door. "You okay?" I set the palm of my hand on her forehead. Her skin's clammy.

"I'm fine, sweetheart." Her voice always rises when she's ducking the truth. "We were just having coffee. Talking about old times."

I push past her with Irene stepping on my heels.

A thin-lipped, guilty-looking man is sitting at the table, shirt open to show off a mat of brown chest hair that stops suddenly at the base of his naked neck. Happy's resting her black muzzle on his thigh. Labs will go whoring for a pat on the head.

Mom tightens the belt on Dad's bathrobe. "Lillian, I'd like you to meet Biff Brookes, a dear old friend of ours from Minnewashka Valley. He dropped by hoping to catch your father at home. Biff, this is my daughter Lillian and this is her friend Irene."

No one moves. Mom looks shell-shocked, and this *Biff* doesn't have the guts to stand up and say hello, but my pal Irene Marlene Patschky is grinning like she just discovered birth control pills.

There is no coffee.

Biff can't help himself a minute longer. He looks at Irene's ankles, then up, over every curve, up five feet, eleven inches until his neck is cricked and his jaw is slack.

Irene arches her back to bring her sizable chest closer to his face, and squinting her already slitty eyes at him, she says, "We don't want to interrupt anything. Lillian and I will go outside and lie down in the sun." She can sweep a room clean of guilt, doesn't matter who owns it or whether they earned it. Usually that's what you want in a friend.

"Too hot around here to lie in the sun," I say. "I mean . . ." I grab Irene's elbow and lift her toward the door. "I mean we're going shopping."

I peel out of the driveway, spitting gravel on Mom's car.

"Cute guy," Irene says.

"Fuck you."

"I just knew old Marion still had it in her."

"You know nothing."

Irene lights two cigarettes and puts one between my lips. "When are you going to learn to relax?"

"Mom thinks she can do whatever she wants," I say. Then I have to stop talking because my breathing's getting ragged and it feels like someone's stepping on my chest. I hand Irene the cigarette and start counting. Fifteen on the intake, fifteen on the out. Nice and steady. The school nurse explained it, talking loud as if I were either deaf or stupid. "You can't just pick one. You have to breathe in *and* out, in *and* out." She's an idiot. At the junction of 42 and 12, I grab a paper bag from my supply in the glove compartment, scrunch a neck into it and put it to my lips while Irene digs through my purse for Tums. It's a little-known fact that they alleviate chest pain. Three miles later, just past the wicked stench of the Kahouts' hog farm, I hand her the bag, she passes me a handful of Tums. Mom discovered Tums. She's another voluntary breather. Upset us and we forget to exhale.

I crank up the radio.

Irene yells over it, "I keep telling you, Lil, you need to teach yourself how to rearrange your thoughts. Maybe you could decide he got there just in time to save her life." She laughs a great whooping laugh as the wind lifts the ends of her hair out the window. "Would you rather have her dead?"

I don't want to admit that I'm not quite that angry. "Not dead. Maybe spayed."

Irene's my only friend for good reason. Say you call some cheerleader at two a.m. to say your dad's trying to lock your mother up in a mental institution. The cheerleader blows it out of proportion—right before she tells her folks. But Irene Patschky asks for every detail, considers it, and outlines her Loose Nut Theory. Nothing you can say will shock her, and she thinks like Dr. Seuss.

I drive the sixty miles to Minneapolis in record time, turning the radio louder and louder, counting phone poles. Fifteen on the intake, fifteen on the out, then a deep hit off a cigarette. The rhythm soothes me. At the shopping center, I drive through the Gopher Lot and park under a big orange sign that says DONKEY LOT, AISLE B.

Inside Woolworth's, I'm drinking Coke from a paper cup, looking at jewelry, when Irene whispers, "Follow me out of the store to the far side of the birdcage." A peroxided Pied Piper. Two weeks ago she'd have been a redheaded Piper. She's the only girl in school who dyes her hair, and she does it the minute the mood strikes. They've stopped sending her home. She wore them out.

In the courtyard of the shopping center, we sit on a wooden bench surrounding a two-story birdcage. When I look at Irene I laugh, even though I don't want to.

"You need earrings," she says in her fortuneteller's voice.

"No shit, Sherlock. Add a rich father to the hit list."

She shakes her hand to make her armload of bangle bracelets clatter. "He's not in your pocket, but the earrings are."

A small white card holding perfect imitation gold hoops is in my pocket. "What the hell did you do?" I shove them deep into my purse. But a minute later I see her point. This could turn the day around. It makes sense. I ease them back out, and keeping them down next to my hip, I take a look. God, they're great. Shiny gold tubes, wide at the bottom, narrowing at the top, the kind worn by rich girls with thick, bouncy hair. "But they're for pierced!" I look up at the birds. A white parakeet chases a blue one, both flying small circles up in the top of the narrow cage. Count the birds. You don't cry over stolen earrings. Two green birds, four yellow.

Irene elbows me. "Look." In the palm of her hand sits a packet of darning needles and a spool of black coat thread. "It's simple." Everything's simple for Irene. When she pierced her own ears at nine, the town buzzed for weeks. She's wearing tarnished wire hoops now. "It won't hurt. Mine hurt because I didn't use ice."

Sitting on a sink in the ladies' room in the basement of the shopping center, I hold paper towels under my chin to catch the drips from the ice cubes Irene is pressing to either side of my right earlobe. Every few minutes, she takes a sip of Coke, spits fresh ice cubes into her hand and replaces the melting ones at my ear.

I take a long drag off a Kool, then hold the cigarette to her lips. "Feels completely dead to me," I say through the smoke, wondering what the needle will feel like.

She drops the ice into the sink and draws a spot on my wet earlobe with a red pen.

"Just do it," I say, "but be careful you don't jam that needle into my neck."

The crunching sound is more surprising than the slight prick followed by a dull ache. As Irene pulls the needle, I watch the thick black thread from the corner of my eye, inching up to where it disappears right into me. I take a hit off the remains of the cigarette and hold the smoke in until it moves around deep in my lungs like a warm cloud.

Irene leaves the thread hanging from my right ear while she pierces the left. When she's done, I turn and stare in the mirror. My long red hair is tucked behind my ears. I've started thinking lately that my ears aren't all that big, they just sit on my head at an odd angle. Under the cheap overhead light I'm almost invisible—blond eyebrows, white skin. But the heavy black thread hanging from either earlobe looks as bold as the Sioux war bonnets at Fort Snelling. There are only a few drops of blood. We froze the rest.

Irene looks at my ears with pride as she releases the gold hoops from the card.

The earrings feel wonderfully heavy, hanging from my ice-cold earlobes. I tilt my head from side to side. They slap my jaw-bone. I raise my arms, snap my fingers and shimmy, catching the glint that comes from me now when I move. I jump down from the sink. "Meet me back here in twenty minutes."

Woolworth seems brighter this time. I look at eye shadow and lipstick. I chat with the fat brunette girl restocking the rack, and when I think she might recognize my stolen earrings, I smile to let her know I can be trusted. Half an hour ago I could have. She smiles back. I turn slowly, making a complete circle in the middle of the aisle, filling up with the freedom of knowing I can have anything I want as long as it's small enough. I pay fifty-nine cents for a plastic hand mirror and wander back past the jewelry, easing the staple from the bag. I lean in to study some earrings, palm a pair like the ones bobbing in my ears, slip them into the bag and walk out the door, my heart pounding nicely. I can feel the color pulsing in my cheeks.

Ten minutes later, Irene appears in the ladies' room, wearing a scoop-necked pink polyester shell—the good kind that hardly ever needs ironing. When I give her the earrings, she throws her old ones in the trash barrel, one at a time, over her shoulder, without even looking.

"Why's this so easy?" I ask. I'm sitting on the sink again while she puts red lipstick on me.

"Because no one cares?" She holds the end of my chin up with her baby finger, squinting with the effort of staying in the lines. "See?" she says. "Look in the mirror. Redheads can wear red lipstick. Red goes with red."

On me it looks like blood. I wipe it off with toilet paper and tell her thanks anyway.

"Where'd you get the shell?" I ask.

I take six shells into the dressing room in Davidson's Department Store. As I tuck one into my purse, a saleslady asks through the curtain whether I need help. She calls me *dear.* "No thanks. I'm doing fine all by myself." Fifteen on the intake. "I have everything I need."

In the lingerie department, Irene and I walk out of the dressing room wearing three bras apiece, one on top of the other. We buy a pair of knee-highs and have the claw-fingered saleslady put them in a large shopping bag. With a handle, please. On the third floor we fill it with skirts and a paisley scarf that looks like silk.

"Let's make a rule," I say. "Every time we fill this bag, we'll empty it into the trunk of my car. That's the safest way." We change clothes lying down on the car seats, and I sail back into the shopping center wearing a white culotte dress that makes me look perfectly thin. Irene's wearing Cover Girl Precious Pink lipstick and shorts that match the pink shell so well it looks like a whole outfit.

We fill the bag again, then rent a locker to save the walk to the car. We have to pay for hot dogs, but I sneak two bags of chips from the metal rack so we'll be constantly gaining ground.

At the birdcage, we rest, smoking cigarettes. "I should get Mom a birthday gift," I say. "She'll be forty-three next week."

"She has pierced ears, right?"

"Yes, but she can go straight to hell. Let's do our Christmas shopping."

After a visit to the drugstore, I draw a chart on a tablet, wishing I had a ruler so I could put the names and gift ideas into little boxes with spaces to check off when we've gotten the gifts. But it's hard to hold the tablet, smoke a cigarette and write while you're sitting on a slippery bench. My chart's a mess.

"Yoo-hoo, Lillian, it's only May." Irene pulls her hair over one shoulder and starts weaving it into a braid. "We've got too much stuff to hide now."

"But we're only going to do this once. It's illegal, so we have to get it done in one day. That's a rule."

"Name me one of your rules we haven't broken." She's tying a knot in the bottom of the thick braid. She can do a million things with her hair. One minute she's Heidi, the next she's Cher.

"If you don't make up rules, it's like sliding down the rabbit hole. There's nothing to grab on to."

"If I were married to your father, I'd cheat too," she says without looking at me. She's been chewing on it all day.

"Shut up. Just shut up."

"Look at it this way. Good old Jack's always drunk, and he's mean."

"I'll write them both off. So what if she's as bad as he is?"

"Hell, you already know he fools around a lot more than she does."

I stand up and face her. "What about your mom? Like she doesn't drink?"

"Did you ever stop to think that maybe your mom only did it this once?"

It hadn't occurred to me that there could ever have been another time.

"And your dad?" I'm hissing like a cat, arms flying around as if they're attached to my words. "What makes your dad so god-damned lily white?"

"Nothing, Miss Lillian. Not a single fuckin' thang." She lines up her ragged sandals and covers her bare knees with the palms of her hands. She stares at the cobblestone floor and says quietly, "Sometimes I think it's Irene here he'd like to fool around with."

I sit down next to her and stare at the spot on the floor that seems to hold her attention. It's all I know how to do.

She stands up and tosses her braid over her shoulder. "Let's go shopping. Who knows? Maybe you've finally made a rule we can keep." She walks off and I realize I don't know if that was Irene, Heidi, Lily Tomlin, Dr. Seuss or someone new. Usually I know when she's slipping around, trying on other people. I do the same and neither of us cares. Other girls expect you to be the same girl all the time.

In Nyberg's Baby Boutique while the salesclerk shows booties to a woman about to give birth, Irene puts our shopping bag on a stroller the way mothers do, and I roll it out into the shopping center. Irene's sister Ava is six months pregnant, and we're throwing the shower.

"Can you still get pregnant when you're forty-three?" I ask.

Irene's quiet for a long time. "No," she says finally. "I'm sure you can't." A few steps later she stops short and looks at me. "Lil. What are you talking about? Your mother had her tubes tied years ago."

It feels like we stole something huge. We race past store windows, pushing the baby stroller, laughing and leaning into each other.

On the up escalator in the middle of the department store, Irene stands backward, holding the front of the stroller while I face her, alert for the exact moment to warn her to step off. I'm thinking it would have been safer to take the elevator, when a tall, skinny man wedges himself onto the narrow step right next to me. I shoot him a dirty look.

"Miss," he says, "at the top of the escalator I'd like you to turn left and go through the green double doors behind men's underwear."

Irene smiles at me. Her eyes are glassy and there's pink lipstick on her front teeth. Blood zips through my veins, whips around the ends of my fingers, up my arms and back into my heart until I'm shaking all over.

She holds one of the double doors open while I push the stroller through, telling myself how smart I am for stashing so much in the locker and the car. When they take this stuff, we'll go home with the rest, so it'll still be progress. And maybe they don't know the clothes in the bag are stolen, and I can say we borrowed the stroller to wheel our package to the car. Maybe they'll let us return it.

Maybe we'll go to jail.

The door closes behind us, and everything's military green, even the pipes running along the walls. You don't realize you've been walking on carpet until you hear your footsteps on cement.

Irene giggles and disappears behind a door with a wire mesh window.

A lady with a jaw slung out like a bulldozer blade directs me toward a matching door on the opposite wall. I try to walk away from the stroller, but she looks at me like I abandoned my child.

"I thought you wanted that," she says in a monotone, then closes the door and pats me down like you see on television. After filling out their perfectly ruled shoplifting inventory form, I put down the pen and sigh with confessional relief.

"Car keys?" she says.

I give them to her.

"Locker key?"

I groan.

Half an hour later two cops come in. "So what did you pick up today?" the chinless one asks, looking at me as if I'm cheap. I look back at him with a little smile, wondering if he noticed the bulldozer jaw on the lady detective.

"Two juvies," she says. "Both claim no priors. Three blouses, six skirts, eighteen greeting cards, a dress, a teddy bear, a lighter, a scarf, cosmetics, cuticle scissors, socks, twelve underpants and a stroller. The stroller's a first."

The fat cop's wide leather belt creaks from the weight of his belly pushing down on a nightstick, handcuffs, a row of bullets and a holster with a gun. I want to explain that they're overreacting; Irene and I aren't real shoplifters. "You can have it all back," I say.

"We do," the lady says.

Irene and I ride behind the steel grate in the police car, heads on our knees so no one sees us. At the station they take mug shots and fingerprints, and leave us in a small room sitting on wooden chairs. Irene lights a cigarette.

"You can't do that here," I say. "We're under age. We don't smoke."

She hands it to me. I take a couple deep drags, hold it out to her, and pull it back for one more puff. "Now put it out," I say. "Just put it out."

"What are they gonna do, arrest us?" She's the bravest girl I know, sitting there in her old brown skirt and her sister's white blouse, raking the braid out of her hair, leaving the bottom six inches rippled. She unbuttons the blouse and leans toward me grinning, tugging on three bras.

The walls of the sergeant's office are covered with rows of photographs of the same two towheaded kids, both wearing his long pointed nose from every angle in every shot. He asks if we understand what we've done wrong. Irene says, "It was the stroller." He says they'll let us go if our parents will come down and sign for us.

"Irene Marlene Patschky," he says, looking at her paperwork.

"Mar-*leeeen*-uh," she says. "You accent the second of three syllables."

He dials the phone and then tosses his booted feet up on his desk. "Mrs. Patschky? Sergeant Johnsson with the Edina Police Department. We are currently detaining your daughter on shoplifting charges."

He stares down his nose at Irene as if he thinks he's single-handedly created the most electric moment of her life.

"Yes, blond . . . Uh-huh . . . Do you have a daughter named Irene? . . . Yes, ma'am . . . I see. God bless. Eleven? Ava, Lana, Greta, Bette, Jayne . . . Tallulah? Yes, I guess you could call Irene a *girl-child*." He takes his feet off the desk and squares his already square body. "With Lillian Anderson . . . Yes . . . Hold on. Amen to you too."

He hands the receiver to Irene, looking sorry he made the call. She gets up from her chair, sits on the edge of his desk, and wiggles around until she's comfortable. She crosses the longest legs Sergeant Johnsson will ever see outside a television screen and tosses her rippled hair over her shoulder before she begins to speak.

"Mom? . . . Yeah . . . yeah . . . shoplifting . . . Just some make-up . . . Can you come and get me? You need to sign . . . Right, *thou shalt not steal.* Mom? Mom . . . where's Dad? Just tell him to. He'll come and get me." She hands the receiver to the sergeant. "My dad's at the feed mill and they don't have a phone. Mom'll send him as soon as he gets back." She lifts one eyebrow. "So Irene will be keeping you company for a while."

He picks up my papers. "Next."

"There's a problem," I say. "My mother has a weak heart. You could kill her with a phone call." I snap my fingers. "Gone!"

"This morning?" Irene says. "This morning an old friend of the family got there just in time. Saved her life."

I can only nod.

The sergeant looks like a man who's had enough of shoplifters and their mothers. He passes me the phone. "You do it."

I stand in front of his desk chewing a hole in the side of my mouth while I count the rings. Eight, nine, no answer. I'm relieved. Ten, eleven. I wonder if she's gone to the Laundro-Matic to cleanse her soul, and suddenly I want to tell her the news. Twelve. She picks up. My mouth goes dry.

"Mom? It's me. Need a big favor."

"What's wrong?" Her voice is chilly because she thinks this is about what she did. The bigger her mistake, the huffier she gets, until it feels like all her mistakes are mine.

"Irene and I are at the Edina Police Station. They want you to come in here and sign some papers."

"Right now? It must be seventy miles."

"Sixty. I'll pay you back." I turn away from the sergeant.

"Honey." Her voice softens. "I've got one of my migraines so bad I can barely see. I have to sit here in the dark until it's gone or it'll kill me."

I cup my hand around the mouthpiece and whisper into the phone. "Did you forget to take your Fiorinal?"

"They didn't do any good."

Irene slides over and puts her ear next to mine, expecting me to turn the receiver so she can hear, but I hold it tighter.

"Mom . . ."

"Fiorinal can't fix everything."

"Listen to me. For once? Will you? If you don't sign some papers, they'll put me in jail." Irene wraps her hair around her neck, pulls it up like a hangman's noose and sticks out her tongue.

"Sweetheart, nobody will put you in jail. Just tell them I always let you sign my name."

"We've been *arrested* by the *police* for *stealing*."

"Can't Irene's mother sign?"

"Mom. Just do it and we'll call it even."

She starts to cry, dissolving on me like a wet paper towel. "This pain in my head could cause a car accident."

"You're the one who belongs in jail."

I hear her breath catch, but I can't stop. "Why can't you act like a normal parent?"

I hear her trying to inhale as she starts to hyperventilate, and her panic flutters inside my rib cage. That's my test—when I can feel it like this, I know she's not faking it. "Mom," I whisper, "breathe *out* first. Then you can breathe in." She wheezes like the air brakes on a semi. "*Mom.* I love you, Mom. You know that. Mom. We're going to be fine. Count with me. We'll do fifteen out, then fifteen in."

Safety Off, Not a Shot Fired

Jack & Marion are celebrating
Their 22nd wedding anniversary!!!!!
But we need Help!!!!!
Saturday
7:30 on the dot!
For skinny-dipping, cha-cha-cha-ing
And Marion's Famous Norwegian Spaghetti!
B.Y.O.B.
Just like it used to be!!!!!!!

Last year my English teacher said, "Lillian, your mother has bursts of vigor." Well, a burst of *something* hit her so hard just now it launched her like a bottle rocket, up onto the back of the davenport where she's standing with her back to me and her nose to the picture window, still wearing the yellow damask short shorts and matching midriff top she made from leftover drapery fabric on Tuesday. When she reaches sideways, I notice the tiny mound of tuna salad on her finger, and I relax, thinking she's just up there trying to coax the crow off the valance. But then she says over her shoulder, "I'm going to throw a big party. A big, big party."

"You don't want a party," I say, hoping Rastus doesn't crap

down the window again. But the foot-tall black bird hops neatly onto her finger and she spins to face me, smiling as if I'd doubted he'd obey.

"Your father's back on the wagon," she says. "We've made up. We're starting over. It's a clean slate for both of us."

The look on my face would knock her to the floor if the vigor weren't making her strong, but her chin's high, posture's perfect, curly blond hair is under control—hair so thick she takes the thinning shears to it.

She says, "He promised from now on he'll only drink beer. Your father is on the wagon."

"Are you kidding? Are *you kidding*? What, the *beer* wagon?" She believes anything anyone tells her, as if the last liar in America was hunted down and hanged the night before she was born.

"You're no fun." She jumps off the davenport, Rastus riding her finger. "You were my most serious baby."

"I don't mean to tell you how to run your life, but get a pencil. Take some notes."

She opens the screen door, tosses Rastus into the night like her old black cape and comes back in. "Remember how I used to love to dance? Best dancer in my class. The lindy, the cha-cha." She grabs my hands. "One, two, cha-cha-cha." What she loves is wiggling her body around while people watch.

I jerk my hands away. "I'll give you three good reasons not to have a party. One: You can't get this house clean in six days. Two: If it rains for more than twenty minutes, the roof will leak, the basement will flood, the water pump—"

"Someday you'll trip over your tongue from talking too fast." She always says that.

"—the water pump will burn out, the toilet won't flush and no one will notice how well you do the damned cha-cha."

I hate the sounds of water moving—toilets flushing; hundred-proof Old Heaven Hill knocking ice cubes against the glass; water dripping off icicles, free-falling two stories to hit the frozen ground like marbles, finally seeping through the walls and trickling into the basement. I hate the sounds of men peeing followed by the wild sucking sounds of the flush. I even hate the tiny carbonated pops of snow melting.

"Number three," I say. "Only one burner works, the oven's dead and Dad won't give you a nickel to get anything fixed."

"You forgot." She grins, and shakes her finger at me. "The *trailer* stove still works."

I swallow number four, which is that everyone in Acorn Lake will stampede down our road to see how far we've slid. As if they don't already know.

She stays up all night writing lists: guest lists, to-do lists, to-buy lists. She loves making lists—like writing it down is getting it done. She writes invitations too, a teetering stack: white ink on slabs of black construction paper. "Fifty-seven," she says the next morning, sitting on the edge of her chair, smoking, tapping her tiny feet to complete silence.

"Suicide notes. Fifty-seven suicide notes."

"The best people in town." Meaning the ones who stopped inviting Mom and Dad because Dad won't leave before breakfast the following day.

"I can't be there. Irene and I have plans."

The first guests arrive stone-cold sober at seven-thirty on the dot to find Mom at the door, back arched, slippery silver pants looking sprayed on instead of sewn up by her last night to show off her perfect body. I'm dressed tastefully in high-necked baggy beige clothing carefully chosen to balance her off, and Dad's stark naked because the slow-moving son of a bitch is still upstairs in the shower, making the water pipes shriek like the brakes on the Northern Pacific going through town. Noises shoot through our house as if it's a two-story tent with blanket walls. Dad never thought about building it to last. Hell, he accuses Mom of thinking too much, like it can blind you.

When I squint, the house doesn't look so bad. I tucked the furniture throws in to fit tighter than Mom's silver pants and removed every light bulb except two dusty forty-watters. After Davey helped her roll up the Early American rug, they hand-rubbed dance wax on the tile floor and tossed down a light coat of sand. The Best Dancer in Her Class says sand is the secret to the cha-cha.

I jump when Joe and Peggy Hearse push past us into the living room without a word, as if being a housepainter gives him inspection rights. I look wherever they look—baseboards, paneling, high-beamed cathedral ceiling—before I realize I'm squinting and they're not.

I promised Mom I'd stay here until Dad comes down. Then it's white lipstick, black eyeliner, midnight-blue mascara, and lickety-split into my new peasant blouse and the magic bell-bottoms that erase my hips. My boyfriend moved to Owatonna six days ago and hasn't called since, so I'm meeting Irene at an island party thrown by city boys. You can do whatever you want out there; that's why it's called an island. Besides, we'll all be doing the cha-cha by the time Acorn Lake's only cop gets a boat—even though two kids drowned there in '63 doing it hanging under a pontoon boat. Farm kids should stick to haylofts.

Mom threads her arm through mine like I'm her date, and I

step back into the shadows, glad to be wearing clothes the color of pine paneling.

Island parties start late, but I could be waiting in my bedroom with the ripple chips and the Reader's Digest Condensed Book that appeared in the mailbox, unordered, unpaid-for. I'm reading *Airport*. With all the blah-blah-blah parts cut out, you can read a book a day. They should write them that way in the first place. What a waste.

I don't have to stand here feeling like this is my ratty house and my missing husband. I catch myself sucking in my stomach, then realize I'm not the one wearing pants that fit like Saran Wrap.

People keep coming. Mr. Towney needs mouthwash. Mrs. Kahout's pregnant. Nothing changes. Mom elbows me to notice Mrs. Christian's long skirt, but I'm smiling into the pink face of Officer Sunny Burger, a man in civvies, a cop without a boat.

The living room fills fast with cigarette smoke, sugary perfume, and women with gooey pink lipstick, vinyl handbags, and wrinkles visible from fifteen feet in forty watts. You wonder why people don't stay home once they look like that. Frank Sinatra's singing that soon I'll see a stranger across a crowded room. And he's right. These men are wearing white patent-leather belts, matching shoes, matching bellies. God, I hope they're not still having sex. The prompt ones. The invitees. The sober seven-thirty-on-the-dotters.

Davey's wearing a white shirt I've never seen before. It's tucked into a belt, his hair's Brylcreemed off his face, and there's a dish towel draped over his elbow. He stops in front of Bung Gunderson, holding up a tray of Mom's chopped-Spam, hot-cheese and Hi Ho appetizers, but Mr. Lazy Acres Beach and

Campgrounds waves him away like cigar smoke. I take a cracker, lean close to Bung and say, "THANK YOU VERY MUCH, DAVEY." Davey might be a pain in the ass, but in this crowd he's on my team and his assignment is appetizers. When his tray's empty, he'll slip outside, run around the dark side of the house to the driveway and get more from the trailer's tiny oven. All Mom will have to do is sneak out there at eight forty-five, pop garlic bread into the oven, heat vegetables, and boil noodles.

"Hey, hey," Dad shouts from behind me in his warm baritone.

"Hey, hey," everyone shouts back, swiveling to greet Good Old Jack.

He stays on the wide bottom step. It only lifts him from five-seven to five-ten, but with his white-blond hair and powder-blue eyes, wearing his burgundy sport shirt, madras pants, patent-leather belt and matching shoes, with his fat silver ring with the chunk of real turquoise, he stops people in their tracks. Slays them. He raises his arms and they're quiet. He salutes them with his highball glass, and the noise returns as if the starting gun went off.

I catch Mom's eye and point the tip of my nose at three inches of Old Heaven Hill in Dad's glass. That's bourbon. Rot-gut. Cheap-as-they-come. It's not-beer. It is not *on the wagon.* The sides of Mom's mouth fold down so fast you might think she's kidding.

Next to me, Davey offers appetizers to Luella Malarkey who's too busy studying the furniture to notice. I whisper, "Go stir the spaghetti sauce." The pot's been bubbling on the single working burner all day. "Just keep stirring."

Mom's looking at the ceiling with her mouth wide open, trying to get a grip. This could go either way, but she recovers so fast it's as if someone blew air into her valves. She straightens up, kicks off her strappy high-heeled sandals and leaps onto the bottom step next to Dad like a Rockette—like Peter Fucking Pan in sprayed-on pants—shouts, "Happy anniversary," wraps her arms around his neck and kisses him. With her back to the audience, she rises onto her toes and wiggles her bottom like her waist is hinged. God, don't you hate to see your parents kiss? It's worse when other people see it, even worse when they drag it out. Dad's dragging it out . . .

Until the whole damned town goes, "Ahhhh. Ohhhhh! Ha-ha-ha!" Then some moron in the back—Butch Malarkey, I think—says, "Jack! Jack! Jack!" And everybody claps to the beat. God, they're all chanting.

It's only eight-thirty.

Dad bends her backward for an old-fashioned movie kiss, she flops her arms out to show us she's helpless to his charms—and knocks the highball glass from his hand. It hits her shiny tile floor with a crash, launching splinters through the cha-cha sand, and everyone—the invitees and the uninvited—jumps as far away as they can.

"Oh, for Chrissake, Marion," Dad says, still holding her bent over backward on the step. She looks confused, hanging there limp, looking at people upside down. Then he lets her go. I try to race toward her, but it feels as if I'm running across the bottom of the deep end of the lake while I watch her eyes flicker from surprised to stricken, her hands rise to cover her face and then swing back down to catch her on the edge of the step as she tumbles to the floor. Before I can reach her, she stands, takes two steps in the broken glass and starts to fall again. This time I catch her.

Hanging heavy in my arms, she says to Dad, "I thought you were supposed to hold me up."

He looks around the room, palms up, as if he's putting it to a vote.

"Broom?" Joan Hansen says. She jerks open a closet door, releasing a long string of falling-down sounds as everything we thought we'd hidden—vacuum parts, cane poles, cleaning rags, a flashlight, the pellet gun, half a dozen arrows, a ball of cat fur and a can of Rust-Oleum—*everything* cascades into the living room. When it finally seems to be over, the aluminum minnow bucket bounces off the top shelf, clatters onto the tile floor and rolls to the center of the room, where it does a slow spin in the cha-cha sand.

In the bathroom, I settle Mom on the closed toilet and kneel at her feet. As I struggle to find the sparkle of glass in the light from a single bulb, she says, "But he's on the wagon." While I paint her soles with Mercurochrome, she says, "He shouldn't have had that highball." As I bind her feet in bandages, I hear Dad through the door, laughing, making sure everyone gets a fresh drink and that it's from their own bottle. I imagine him smiling, shaking hands, saying thanks when they wish him happy twenty-second, like he got here alone. Mom says, "I'm not going to speak to him for a month of Sundays."

"That'll work."

By the time Mom and I come out, Good Old Jack has lifted the party up off the floor, easy as raising a pup tent—but that shouldn't be a surprise. You can't keep Jack Anderson down. Hell, everybody in Sioux County heard about the time he passed out, toppled backward off his snowmobile at three a.m. doing sixty-five across Highway 16, spent an hour lying spread-eagled in the fast lane, snowmobile in the ditch, huge middle-of-the-night trucks zooming around him until someone must have decided he was human and not some overstuffed garbage bag and called the police. Officer Sunny Burger woke him up, brought him home and stayed until they'd finished the quart of sloe gin that had survived the crash.

That night there were twenty guys ahead of Dad in his barhopping snowmobile posse, twenty guys and Bettina Boop. "*Betty* Boop to you, honey," she likes to say, walking into the VFW, unzipping her yellow snowmobile suit like a woman peeling a banana. "Boop-boop-ee-doop!" She'll pose by the cigarette machine, all tits and hips—that old-fashioned hourglass shape old men love. Betty's famous. Her silver silhouette's on the mud flaps of every eighteen-wheeler that ever blew you off the road on a rainy night. Everyone in town knows about her. Her and Dad.

Mom and I watch Davey sweep the last shards of glass into the dustpan. He must have jammed all our stuff back into the closet—except the minnow bucket that's sitting on the coffee table under his empty tray. Mom and I smell the spaghetti sauce burning and race for the kitchen. We're at the stove, keeping the burned sauce on the bottom of the pot while we drain the good part into mixing bowls when we hear it: "Boop-boop-ee-doop!"

Mom's hands fly up and cover her mouth as if the sound came from her. "We were starting over," she says through her fingers as tomato chunks and ground beef fall from the wooden spoon in her hand and bounce down the front of her pants. She's crying hard, hands crossed over her chest now as if she's trying to hold her heart in.

"Let's go to the trailer." I pry the spoon from her fingers.

She shakes her head.

"Don't let them see you like this."

"No!" she says, pulling away from me. "I'm *going* into *my* living room."

I bear-hug her and whisper, "We'll go out to the trailer and cook the food. Then, if you want to come back, we'll come back." It can't be a hundred feet from the kitchen, around the dark side of the house and out to the driveway, but with her crying and hobbled, it takes forever.

Less than two hours into their twenty-second wedding anniversary party, Mom says she's decided to kill Dad one day soon.

"Dibs on his binoculars," I say and dump more Worcestershire sauce in the Chex party mix. She can't kill him. He's too mean to die.

We're standing hip to hip on the slanted floor of Dad's trailer-house, right legs higher than our left, leaning south together because his two-wheeled tin can is resting forward on its hitch. We're working by the moonlight flooding over the café curtains, with the windows shut so the guests won't smell food and realize we have to cook in the driveway.

Davey pops his head in the door and says with false calm, "We are now out of food." I replace his tray with a bowl of party mix and he disappears.

It's so hot in here my bra is suctioned on, and at ninety percent humidity, every smell hits as hard as a hammer. There's garlic and yeasty sourdough bread, melted butter, lots of mold, Worcestershire sauce, the leftover tang of unwashed hunters, and a strong undertow of dead ducks—a deep swampy smell. I slide a window open.

"I mean it," Mom says. "I'm figuring out how to kill him."

On an up day she's twice as smart as he is. But she can't kill him. Hell, you could throw my dad into a raging river and he'd float faceup, lying so high in the water that the Camels in his shirt pocket wouldn't get wet. Over the falls, between the rocks, a man saved so goddamned many times you'd think he'd have started believing in God. I asked him about God once—just the two of us in his car, coming back from nowhere. "Oh for Chrissake!" he said, gruff, as if I'd quizzed him about Betty Boop.

Now cars and pickups are sitting every which way in the field across the road. I slice a radish into a rose, listening to missing tailpipes and glass-packs and mufflers with holes the size of cows. They're parking in our yard like tires don't kill grass. Ten minutes ago I counted seventy-seven people spilling from the living room down the lawn onto the dock. People always head for the lake as if water will change something.

"Better move it, Mom. They're running out of food."

She pauses in a moonbeam, knife in midair.

"Or," I say, "we can stay in here until they leave. Either way is fine."

Her eyes lock on the green vinyl banquette heaped with hunting magazines, hip boots and the empty motor oil cans we moved to clear a path through the rolling trash can Dad calls his *rig*. "I couldn't do it before," she says, "but I can kill him now." A sweat bead rolls off her forehead. I've never seen her this way, face so puffed with rage, she might be wearing the skin of a much smaller woman. She turns away, clumsy on bandaged feet, and starts scraping the burned bottom off the bread like sharpening a knife on a stone.

"Mom?"

"How?" She stomps her foot and folds in pain. "How could he do this? Inviting Betty into my house on our anniversary? Now I *have* to kill him. You understand, don't you?"

Dad deserves to die, so I don't mention that Betty might have invited herself. "You'd get caught if you shot him."

"Who would believe I could kill someone? If I back the car over him, a hundred people could testify that he always said I don't know my rear end from my front."

"Nah. He'd live another fifty years. *Marion! Oil my wheelchair. Hey! Slow the hell down. Not that slow. For Chrissake, can't you even push a goddamned wheelchair?*"

"Poison?"

"He'd throw it up like a hair ball."

"Brake lines?"

"Nah. Jail time. A hundred people could testify you had a hundred motives."

Without warning, the trailer door opens and Betty Boop comes up the stairs as if she's always known exactly where we were. When she pauses on the top step and holds out a pack of Kools, I'm so surprised I take two and hand one to Mom.

"Sorry, girls, I'm fresh out of matches." She hands me her lit cigarette. Her voice is husky and even in this summer heat, she smells like burning leaves, like late October. I light our cigarettes off hers. Her long curly black hair is piled on top of her head in a perfect mess—and she's wearing a peasant blouse and bell-bottoms. She nods once at me, then looks Mom in the eye. "That old tight-ass Luella Malarkey just told me it's your anniversary. Couldn't wait to say it."

I've passed Betty Boop on the street and seen her in the grocery store, but I've never had a chance to stand this close and stare. She's not fat for her age, but her chin has a dimple so deep it looks like a baby's ass, and her lips are so round and pink they might have been blown out of bubblegum. Everything about her is round—cheeks and chin and the cleavage busting out of her blouse. But she's got a nose straight as a ruler and squared off at the tip.

Mom sniffles and dabs her own tiny nose with the back of the hand still holding the knife.

"Awww, Christ," Betty says. "Jack nearly wrenched my arm off, never said a word about it being your anniversary. *I* know—" She lifts her hands to protect her face, like Mom has a history of fistfights. "You're right. Shouldn't have come anyway." Her blue eyes are so big they're just this side of bulging. You'd expect lots of makeup, but she probably knows people don't look at her face. She shrugs. "I know what you think of me, Marion, but I'm not low enough to wreck your damned wedding anniversary." She takes a deep breath and relaxes into the exhale as if that finishes it, then looks around. "Man oh man. Look at this place. Jack's a real pig, isn't he?"

"No kidding," I say.

Mom's teary. "He's a wonderful man."

"Honey, I'm really sorry." Betty says it to Mom, and it feels like I've been cheated on and now I'm being pitied by Bettina Boop.

"Keep the bastard," I say.

She shakes her head. "I can't believe I let him convince me to come to your goddamned *house*." She leans down the steps to prop the door open and comes back bringing a fresh breeze. "Sure's shooting I'll find tons of new mistakes to make, but I promise you I'll never make this exact one again."

Mom nods, sniffling, believing every word. "Oh, Betty," she says, "Jack and I were starting over."

"Right after we killed him," I say. "We were deciding how to do it when you invited yourself in here."

"Judas priest, girls. Just don't get caught. Some men are worth jail time and Jack's not one of them."

I'm sixteen years old, standing in the near-dark in a smelly trailer-house on a Saturday night, wearing high-necked baggy beige clothes, dripping sweat, and agreeing with every word Betty Boop says.

Mom says, "He's worth it."

"What?" I ask.

"I couldn't have been married for twenty-two years to a man who's not worth it."

I say, "Should have killed him right after I was conceived."

Betty laughs and leans against the top bunk bed. "Let you in on a little secret." She takes a drag off her cigarette and blows out the smoke. "When my Freddie died so young? No time to even have a kid. Shit, I thought it was all over for me."

Mom nods, "I thought so too. Everybody said so."

"But if I'd known then what I know now, I might have killed him myself."

Mom says, "Betty!"

I laugh and it feels like another window slid open.

"Yes, ma'am. You're looking at a girl who needs lots of time alone."

Mom says, "Nobody wants to be alone."

"Freddie wanted me with him every minute—watching football, washing his car. The man couldn't take a piss by himself. But he could go for days without saying a word to me. Then the second I phoned a friend, his mouth would fall open and words would flow out until I hung up." She looks me in the eye. "Those were the loneliest years of my life."

"There are good men out there," Mom says like she's got proof.

"I like being alone," Betty says. "I enjoy it. Add to that I'm a lousy cook and can't sew a stitch."

Mom says, "You could learn . . ."

"Honey, once you learn how to cook and sew, hordes of hungry men will show up on your doorstep dragging gunnysacks full of mending."

"I don't sew," I say.

Betty checks her watch. "Time for me to get out of your lives."

Mom says softly, "You don't have to leave." She shrugs. "Everybody in America already knows you're here."

"Mom." I make my eyes wide, trying to get her to pay attention for once. Nodding, I say, "If she wants to leave, we should *let* her leave."

Mom brushes the air with her hand. "Betty and I knew each other long before you were born."

Slugged by fatigue, I sink onto the bottom bunk.

Betty seems to think about it while she blows a narrow tube of smoke and watches it follow the low ceiling toward the back of the trailer before doglegging left to stream out the open window. She looks down at me. "This woman in the paper once? Sets the vacuum cleaner in the water where her husband's standing washing his new Firebird. Plugs it into one of those outside plugs. *Zzzzzztt!* Fries him."

"She get away with it?"

"Yup." She looks around again, wrinkling her straight nose. "Jack's a real pig. I should've left him lying on his back in the fast lane."

· · ·

Word of the party must have blown through every bar in town, and by ten-thirty people are clustered on our patio, shiny-eyed, gazing past each other, then back over their shoulders, looking for something. They're in the living room, liquor bottles tucked up hard into their armpits, cigarettes burning to the filter. This isn't the best people in town; this *is* the fucking town. Some brought cases of beer and even those who didn't know the invitation said B.Y.O.B. brought their own because Jack never bought a drink for anyone and no one wants to be caught dry when Bobby's Liquor closes Saturday night and stays closed until Monday. The invitation should have said *Bring Your Own Food.*

I'm in the kitchen, filling plates with sweet rolls, sliced bananas, potato chips. Anything I can find. I bury toast triangles in grape jelly because running out of food is worse than getting cheated on.

I can hear Mom and Betty in the living room. They're working opposite sides of the crowd, just happening to mention that Mom invited her old friend Betty to her party. "First one on my list," Mom says again. And Betty says even louder, "Best damned dancer in our class. Remember?"

In ten minutes I'm heading for the real party—where nobody knows anybody and no one's from here. I can almost feel the cool air and hear waves slapping the bow of the boat. *That's* a water sound I like, that and the sound of the bathtub filling up.

When the music blares, I peek around the corner. Mom's standing in front of the hi-fi with her back to the room, head down, shoulders rising as if she's sucking life from the neck of a song, stealing it from Louis Prima and Keeley Smith. *"Closest to the bone, sweeter is the meat."* Her back is still to the crowd when she starts moving her hips, getting into it with her shoulders, head swaying so loose her neck might be a wire. *"The last slice of Vir-*

ginia ham is the best that you can eat . . ." She pivots neatly on bandaged feet, flips her head up, and with her party face back on, she looks at the entire town.

And Dad shouts, "Marion, baby!"

As the crowd between them clears, Betty nods at me from across the room and disappears out the door.

Mom puts her hands behind her head and presses her elbows back. Dad sets his drink down, and with his hands in the air and his fingers snapping, he dances toward her—everybody watching, quiet from the power of it. He slips a little on the waxed tile, recovers, takes a step to the right and dances toward her again, singing softly. *"Closest to the bone . . ."* He comes toward her. *"Sweeter is the meat . . ."* He takes a step backward. A step forward. Like he's teasing her.

She stands in front of the hi-fi on bandaged feet, unable to dance toward him, but moving, shimmying, drawing him toward her. No one says a word, although Peggy Hearse purses her lips and elbows Luella Malarkey who nods and purses her own lips. Mom *licks* her lips, tucks her chin into her neck and looks out the top of her eyes at him while her arms reach for him, rippling like long weeds in shallow water, calling him in.

He slows for a second, shakes his head like an angry bull, then dances forward, head down, trying, he's trying to get to her. He looks up and smiles at her, his face full of love, just like it used to be, then lurches to the right, lurches to the left and falls to the floor like a tree.

She stares down at him, eyes wide, then seems to remember that her arms are still reaching for him and drops them to her sides. A quick laugh slips from her, she lifts her chin, tilts her head, smiles, shakes her head, shrugs and delivers a ripple of laughs meant to make it look like a lark—but it looks like someone's turning the channel too fast. Dad snorts and she looks down at him one more time.

Inch by inch, she lifts her head. She looks at the people of Acorn Lake as if they're strangers on a street corner in downtown Minneapolis, then steps over Dad, and with impossibly perfect posture, hobbles to the stairs. One by one she climbs them, her head high and her son at her heels, his dish towel still draped across his bent elbow.

You could toss my dad off a ten-story building and he'd bounce right back up. He loves telling about the time he dozed while hunting, fell thirty feet off a tree stand, woke up cradled by a snowdrift, shotgun between his legs like a witch's broom, safety off, not a shot fired.

As I stand here in the corner of the living room watching the crowd, the rain starts ticking against the windows like fingernails. The guests are still gathered in groups, swapping stories, glittery-eyed, like people who've seen a train wreck, each one hoping to report something no one else saw, all of them looking well fed.

I hear the rain on the roof now. Won't take much of this to chase the city boys back to the city or to drive Rastus back inside. Whenever the front door opens, I imagine him swooping in here and circling the room, bringing these people to their knees with his surprising burst of blackness. But crows are clever and Rastus comes and goes as he pleases.

Dad's on his feet again. He found his empty glass and he's holding it above his open mouth, waiting for one last drop when the rain starts tapping harder on the roof. He stands there, open mouth turned toward the cathedral ceiling as the tapping grows steadily to a pounding, then a drumming, then a hammering so loud you can picture the water rolling and tumbling, fighting its way under loose shingles, sheeting off the roof, pooling in the yard, working its way down into the soil at the edge of the house, seeping in through the foundation.

Pixie Dust

I'm lying in bed, face to the wall, already knowing everything worth knowing. Nothing more I want to do or say or go to, no one I want to meet. The only trip I want to take is from my right side to my left. And Mom's coming down the hall singing that I should just call her *angel of the morning*.

My door opens. She's in here. She sits down, shaking my bed, and I roll toward her, snarling. She's got a glass of V-8 in one hand and a bullet-sized black capsule in the other. "Come on, Lily Nilly. Take this and I promise your mother will be gone with the wind."

"Go away." I flop an arm over my face. I have always been a napper, but two months, two weeks and six days ago my boyfriend, Stash, moved to Owatonna, and he hasn't called yet. I am now the Queen of Sleep. At lunch, in class, or in the library reading a book, my eyes slam shut, my head falls forward like a granite ball and I sleep until someone makes me move. I gave up going to school on Fridays weeks ago. Now I skip Wednesdays too. Last week I didn't go at all.

Mom is singing, "*I love YOUUUUUUU, a bushel and a PECK, a bushel and a PECK, and a hug around the neck, and a BAR-REL . . .*" I moisten the capsule on my tongue, swallow hard and turn my blanketed back to her. "Dahhhh-dahh-DEE, *a bushel and . . .*"

Fifteen minutes later I pop up like toast, peel my nightgown over my head, fold it into a six-inch square, and am about to put it in my dresser when I notice my underwear drawer is a jungle, so I fold everything in all six drawers with marching-band precision, then rush to sort the mountain of clothes from my closet floor into three piles: washing, ironing, and good-enough-to-wear-again. Suddenly I understand logic, I understand order, and it gives me a new kind of pleasure to introduce them both to my closet. My closet matters.

Two hours later, chain-smoking, still buck naked, I strip the bed and turn the mattress, top to bottom, then end to end, thinking that'll make it last forever. I'm extending the life of this mattress out so far that I can see myself sleeping on it with gray hair. Progress is everything. I dress from the dirty pile so I'm not losing ground. What a girl I am.

Finally.

By four-forty Saturday afternoon, I've been doing projects in my room for thirty-three hours and forty minutes. Better yet, I haven't eaten a crumb and I can feel my ribs appearing like the sled after the first false melt in March. I'm at my desk, having finished five chapters in *Gregg Shorthand Made Easy,* enormously pleased by the graceful shapes flowing off the end of my Bic fine-point, red ink on pale green paper, riding the dark blue lines, no margins, not an inch of paper wasted, lighting one cigarette off the other to save matches, when my brain shuts down. I drop the pen, stagger through the washing and ironing piles and flop facedown onto my bare but recently turned mattress.

There's a nail in my right nipple. But I'd remember a nail going in. Wouldn't I? I think my way through it and figure out I'm asleep facedown on a bare bed. I slide my hand in and find the loose mattress button that's carving a hole in me. I roll onto my back. My arms and legs are heavy as fire hoses. I open my eyes. My chest aches from chain-smoking Kools. I'm *hungry.* I drag myself downstairs.

It's Sunday, not yet four a.m., and the living room is lit bright enough to land a plane. We've already had our first hard frost, but every window is open and the temperature can't be over fifty. Davey is sitting on the davenport, zipped to his armpits in Dad's new down-filled mummy bag, his Pop-Tart resting on the floor. He salutes me with his Pepsi bottle and goes back to twirling the knobs of Mitzy's old Etch A Sketch so I don't give him a hard time about eleven-year-olds who stay up all night.

Last year Mitzy drove directly from her Acorn Lake High School graduation to Hollywood, California. Then Randy moved from a tent in Vietnam to a farmhouse in Minnewashka that's filled with vets. Now Davey and I live like two people who missed the last bus out of town. I sleep and he watches reruns of *Ozzie and Harriet,* the *Little Rascals, Sky King*—shows Randy, Mitzy and I watched together when they were new. Once at three a.m. I found Davey alone in the living room with the projector set up, looking at slides of the three of us from before he was born. With the color from the screen reflecting on his face, he asked me why Mom waited so long to have him, and I said, "It's the middle of the night."

Now Mom is standing where the kitchen opens onto the living room, barefoot and tiny in red shorts and a tank top, cigarette clenched between her lips so she can use both hands to smooth the wrinkles out of a wide piece of walnut-colored wood-grained Con-Tact paper she's applying to the rusty refrigerator door.

"Move." I tug the door open to get the milk.

"Good morning!" A sweat bead rolls off the end of her nose. She's been dripping for months, probably thinking about *Biff.* Her affair was dead for a while, but it's alive again. I just know it. She pulls a strand of hair out of the corner of my mouth, barely missing my eye with the tip of her cigarette.

I push her arm away.

"Isn't it a beautiful day?" she says.

It's still dark out.

I step around her to gather up a bowl, a spoon, the Frosted Flakes and the sugar, intent on eating in bed so I'll already be there when I fall asleep. "Where's Dad?"

"Sleeping."

When he passes out, she gets up and starts her day, usually catching Davey in the wake of her whacked-out schedule. The kid misses more school than I do.

She swaps the carton of regular milk in my arms for a half gallon of skim. "You've got such a good start on a diet," she says, and bows low, one arm across her waist, the other behind her back.

"What the fuck was in that pill?"

"Lillian!"

"What did you give me?"

"Dexedrine."

A new word: Dexedrine. Black capsules filled with pixie dust. Dexedrine.

"They're for my low blood," she says. "When I discovered Dr. Hapley? My hemoglobin was six. Six! Tired as a whipped puppy. But now?" She strikes a new pose, one fist curled in front of her forehead, the other on the back of her skinny hip as if she's a bodybuilder. Her head flips up. "Holy moley, Rocky. Your mother can do anything!"

She embarrasses me even if no one's watching, and then she says it's just my age.

"You've got my low blood," she says. "Dr. Hapley says tired genes run in families. My mother must have had it. Mama was always tired."

I grab a sweet roll from an open package on the dish-strewn counter and head back through the living room, threading my way around her half-done projects. She's braiding a new room-sized Early American rug out of used panty hose. She's painting the brick fireplace navel orange. The clothes dryer's guts are spread out on newspapers. Stuff is everywhere: hunting boots, snow boots, hip boots, waders, and a gunnysack full of goose decoys—the latest lightweight Styrofoam kind—all lying around because she's been hammering together a boot box out of wood she found along the side of the road somewhere.

"Give up!" I shout. "Just give up!"

"Never go upstairs empty-handed," she calls to my back.

I pause long enough to see if my arms are as full of food as I thought.

Early Monday morning Mom drops Dexedrine into my hand like feeding dimes into a candy machine. "Just until you feel good again, honey."

Three hours later I tiptoe into German class, late because I had to shampoo my hair twice, cover each strand with a dab of slippery green Dippity-Do, set it on orange juice cans, and wear the dryer cup while I Windexed every tile on the bathroom wall and scraped the rust from the base of the faucet using the tip of the metal nail file.

"*Guten Morgen,* Fraulein Anderson," Frau Fischer says. For an old woman, she's alert.

I slide into my desk near the back corner of the room.

"*Ach du lieber, heil* Hitler, and what the fuck happened to you?" Irene sits right behind me. "Good hair," she adds. She pulls a curl out straight and lets it go like a spring. I lean back so it's easier for her to reach. When I was little, I'd sit on the floor between Mom's outstretched legs every night while she wound my hair into pin curls and crossed each one with two bobby pins. Suddenly I miss having my hair touched.

I write EAT THIS NOW on a scrap of paper and fold it around a Dexedrine capsule while Frau Fischer stands with one hand inside her navy blue dotted-Swiss dress, absently tugging on her bra strap, lifting one heavy-looking breast, letting it fall, lifting it again. Hypnotizing kids. "*Dürch, für, gegen, ohne, um und wieder* take the accusative." She turns to write on the blackboard, the fat on her back jiggling with each stroke of the chalk. Dexedrine could change her life. She'd still be old, but she'd be thin.

I toss the tiny package over my shoulder. One of the Manson boys sleeping next to us snorts, his face nested deep in his elbows as if he's trying to show off his dirty neck. Tina and Sherry Terry have swiveled sideways in their seats to stare at my hair. In the front of the room, the good kids sit together, writing down everything the Frau says, as if it matters.

Twenty minutes later I'm taking notes for the first time in years when Irene growls: *"Get your motor running."* She kicks the seat beneath me like a drum. "Nah-nah-nah-nah-nah-nah. *Head out on the HIGHWAY."*

"Fraulein!" says Frau Fischer. *"Bitte! Bitte! Bitte!"* But the bell rings and flips the kids right out of their seats.

I buzz through school, turning in overdue work, writing extra-credit papers. Straight-A Student. Learning Machine. Someone Who Cares. One day, sitting in study hall, trying to peel the damned wood-grained Con-Tact paper off my history book, tapping my feet and dying for a smoke, I realize my shoes are loose. I lift a knee and shake my leg around, marveling that even my feet had been fat. Who would have thought of that? Our bathroom scale is broken, but I've been weighing myself anyway, marking my progress on a chart. I've gone from sixty-eight whatevers down to fifty-seven.

I press my thighs against the wooden seat and measure them between my thumb and index finger. Not yet thin enough. I have my arms out straight in front, moving my fingers like a piano player just to see the bones slip around under my skin, when I sense someone watching me. Across the aisle, up one seat, New Kid is looking back with his head tilted, dark eyes glittering behind the gold-tinted lenses of his glasses.

He showed up two years ago, the first new student since third grade, prompting Rat-Face Hanson to shout, "new kid," like it was a scientific sighting. Even the teachers call him New Kid.

He stares at me, wavy black hair looking mysterious in a field of blond kids. There are eighteen boys in my grade and all but Moe and Joey Manson were claimed before we left elementary.

Around here, you don't break up with a boy, you lose your turn—and I have no interest in a used boy. But I failed to consider New Kid. He keeps himself separate. Like me. Now he nods. Barely, and without a smile. High school boys don't nod like that, making my back arch as if he'd run his thumbnail down my spine.

He eases around to face the front of the room, slides down in his desk until his legs are out straight in his khaki pants. He crosses his ankles, and I spend the next twenty-seven minutes studying him, delighted with the way his earlobe angles directly down to meet his jaw rather than jogging up a little first like everyone else's. I want to touch that spot.

The bell rings and he's walking next to me, our arms hinged from shoulder to elbow. We're the same height, so when he turns to face me, our lips are level, his breath is warm on the tip of my nose, and I'm looking through his glasses into magnified eyes. I've never felt this close to anyone. Stash was so tall my face was always buried in the front of his shirt, making it lonely, but I can still feel a cool flat button against my cheekbone, I can smell the Christmas tree air freshener hanging from the rearview mirror in his mother's station wagon, and sometimes I get a whiff of Jade East in the oddest places, but it disappears because I inhale too fast. I thought I loved him, even though most of the time I didn't even like him. But I didn't want him to leave.

New Kid is standing so close that I back into the metal lockers with a loud *vah-woom*. He smiles with one side of his mouth and walks away, leaving me breathless.

"New Kid," I say to Irene that afternoon. I'm lying on one of the wall-to-wall double beds in the farmhouse attic where seven of the eleven Patschky girls sleep. Irene and I cut class so she can try out homecoming hairstyles. I stand up to set the needle back to the start of "Hey Jude" again.

"He's different." She's up for queen. She was princess last year, but she's losing popularity due to cigarettes and sex and a skinny Sioux Indian named Benny Stillwater, losing it to a cheerleader. What's all that damned jumping around good for? You can't eat it, drive it or bank it for later. What a waste.

Irene coils twelve inches of peroxided hair around her fist, lifts it above her head and anchors it with a pair of yellow pencils. The cheerleader is beige and squatty; Irene's the pick of the Patschky litter: Greta, Hedy, Bette, Claudette, Myrna Mae, Ingred, Ava, Lana, Irene, Jayne and Tallulah—every one of them taller than tall, just like their mother, Gula Patschky. After Gula had Tallulah on her forty-third birthday, she started using birth control and going to mass three times a week, either praying the pills would work or apologizing for them.

"New Kid's different," Irene says.

"Moe and Joey Manson are *different*." I lie back down on a bed.

"Anything can be a barrette." She winds a nylon stocking around the tornado of hair and tosses the pencils away like a magic trick.

"Henry *Hoffman* is different," I say.

"You grab whatever you can find and try it."

I pull a Tampax from an open box on the floor and toss it at her. "At least New Kid's fussy. I've never seen him look at another girl."

She rips the wrapper off the tampon, pulls the cardboard tubes apart and strings them like beads over wild shafts of hair. She flashes me a smile. "Why the hell not?"

. . .

On my way to school, I'm stopped at the tracks in my old Chevy, letting the train go by. Finally the caboose rumbles past—revealing the giant bulb-shaped Acorn Lake water tower, where it now says in orange Day-Glo letters: LILLIAN IS FINE '69. He even took time to underline my name. Twice! With a swirl at the end.

At noon he still hasn't come to school. Homecoming festivities have every kid coiled tight as a Slinky anyway, and they're twittering, trying to guess who wrote it. I'm the only Lillian. By twelve-fifteen, bored with looking mysterious, I cut out.

Eighteen-point-six miles of dirt roads follow the winding shores of the lake, most of them dead-ending at creeks or just petering out. I like to follow one to the end, turn around, do the next one, smoking and listening to the radio. I'm singing "Light My Fire" while smoke floats out of my nose and mouth.

Maybe New Kid changed his mind. Maybe he fell off the water tower. Maybe he's dead. I hope he's just letting it simmer. On Dexedrine I can take shorthand at a hundred and thirty words a minute, bob my head, tap my feet, sing "Light My Fire," ride a bicycle and still be thinking about sex. WDGY keeps playing "This Guy's in Love with You." Herb Alpert shouldn't be allowed to sing.

When I get back to town, people are walking to their cars after the homecoming parade, kicking through strips of toilet paper that blew off floats. I pull into the convent parking lot where the parade route ends just in time to see Queen Irene disappear down Main Street on the back of Benny's chopper, her hair like streamers. I'm still smiling when the passenger door opens and New Kid gets in, quiet as a cat and dressed all in black.

. . .

That night we do it in the long dry grass under the football field bleachers, just New Kid and me, again and again, not a word, our bodies striped by moonlight coming through the planks above while giant yellow oak leaves crackle in my hair. Later, lying in the dark, naked under our coats, we share a cigarette and snicker at the chattering kids walking home from the dance. It took the Homecoming Decorating Committee two weeks and forty rolls of crepe paper to turn the gym into Paris. I don't understand what makes them do that stuff. I don't understand.

At two a.m. New Kid drops me off in our driveway, his wet black hair slicked back from his high forehead as if he just showered. Holding my little finger, he says without moving his lips, "Tomorrow." It's the only word he's said so far. He's sophisticated. I think I like not knowing his name.

I go in through the side door, bra in my purse, panties on backward, shoes in my hand, nose tucked into my collar because his warm dark smell rises from my blouse with every step.

In the living room Mom's sitting at the treadle sewing machine her mother passed down. She reaches forward to cut the thread, raising a line of cleavage above her low-necked sweater, and suddenly I'm deeply sorry Grandma didn't also pass along her baggy dresses, her orthopedic shoes and the nylons she darned with black thread. I button the top of my blouse and vow that I will always dress with taste.

Mom looks me over, smiles and lifts her eyebrows with that aren't-we-birds-of-a-feather look, leaving me more naked than I was under the bleachers. I make some rules: I will only have sex once a week, I will never do it again with anyone except New Kid and I will never tell a soul. I drop my shoes and glare at her until her mood changes.

"Your mother has a terrific idea," she says finally, talking about herself as if she's not here. "If you iron your father's shirts, I'll start taking in your clothes." Every day at the last minute, she irons the wrong shirt for Dad. She'll press a short-sleeved shirt when it's twenty below outside or a blue shirt just before he wakes up in the mood for a tan one. And if he has a shirt with ink stains on it, she'll iron that one first and never notice. He'll wave the well-pressed wrong shirt in her face and shout until she weeps, but she still swears that when they were newly-weds she spent every Tuesday pressing his shirts, crying because her heart was bursting with love for him. It always makes my lips curl.

As I fill the steam iron with water, I add ironing to the list of things I will never do for a guy. I've already sworn to myself that I will never cook a meal or sew for a man, never be shouted at in public, never beg for grocery money and I will never ever take a two-week summer vacation in a camper driven by a drunk. I will flat-out refuse to shovel the driveway or the roof and I will never hand a new roll of toilet paper through the bathroom door. Men have got to learn to plan. Even New Kid. Especially New Kid. So maybe I don't love him either.

Mom gives me a Dex from the sewing machine drawer and fifteen minutes later I'm yakking away about how nice she is to share everything she has with me.

"You know you're always welcome to anything that's mine," she says. And it's true. She'd give you the blouse off her back and every coin from her purse before you even thought to ask.

By three a.m. we've removed every lamp shade and it's bright enough for surgery, except where layered clouds of cigarette smoke rise and fall when I reach to hang another shirt on the curtain rod. It's like a Laundromat in our own *Space Odyssey*. Grandma's sewing machine whirs as Mom pumps the treadle. I answer with a hiss of spray starch. We talk to each other for hours like jackhammers breaking up cement, every syllable progress of a sort. I make the shirts smooth. She makes the seams straight and tightens the buttons while I spray-starch the collars.

We talk about clothes and can't agree on what makes a girl look good, so I raise my hands and say *"Fine,"* relaxing into it like the time I learned to slow down and merge behind another car instead of flooring it and praying while my lane disappears.

She tells me about the fifties when doctors gave out uppers to every woman who had a child, saying, *Honey, you girls are all tired.* "Low blood," Mom explains. "You usually get it from having kids." She says they had nursing circles where all her girlfriends would sit around smoking Marlboros, drinking coffee and sharing Dexedrine while they nursed their babies. They laughed a lot and always helped each other out because they loved one another.

Mom and I go back and forth over Dad's drinking as if talking about it long enough will sober him up. She discusses him like he's a lifetime project she has to finish before she dies. We take another Dexedrine. Then she says that my name on the water tower was a declaration of true love.

"Are you in love with him?" She's hoping.

"Nope." I slam the hot iron down on the inside of Dad's collar. I'm sure as hell in something, but I don't want to call it love.

"Love is the most important thing in the world."

"Oh, give me a break. I don't even know his real name."

"Honey, I'll never know what I did to make you so sour, but someday you'll learn that your mother was right. I've lived a lot longer than you have, you know."

"If you could live it all over again but you could change one thing, what would it be?"

"Big breasts." She flips down the sewing machine foot to

anchor the seam of my green skirt, pulls her shoulders back and cups her hands in front of her as if she's holding muskmelons. "I'd have great big breasts."

"Why?" I dream of being chestless, hipless. Twiggy-like.

"Men love big breasts."

"I'd ask for a million dollars."

She laughs. "Girls with big breasts end up getting everything they want."

"I'd rather go straight for the money."

"No. Pick thin, pick thin," she says, bouncing in her chair.

"I'm almost thin now."

"No matter what I eat? I can't seem to gain a pound. Just lucky, I guess."

"You're perfect, Mom."

"No, just naturally thin."

"If you had a million dollars you wouldn't have to be thin unless you wanted to be. You could eat what you wanted to, sleep when you were tired. You could buy a brand-new dryer—" I raise my eyebrows and nod toward the greasy parts lying on the newspapers.

"Big breasts."

"Wait," I say. "Wait. How about a lifetime supply of Dexedrine?"

She shakes her head.

"Don't you want to feel good all the time?"

"Being in love should do that."

"You feel good all the time because you're in love?"

She looks up. Her mouth opens. She blinks.

I push on. "Are you in love?" I haven't said a word since Irene and I caught her here in the middle of the afternoon with Biff. I've been kind enough not to bring it up, but suddenly I want to squeeze it out of her like toothpaste, and I want it to hurt so much she stops acting like a juvenile delinquent. "Hmmmm?"

She cocks her head. "Well, in fact . . ." The sewing machine goes *ticka-ticka* and slows to a stop. Half a breath into the silence I realize she's *dying* to tell me every damned detail about her Biff.

"Wait!" I hold the iron straight out in front of me with both hands. "Stop."

"Certain lovers were meant to be together."

"No."

"We can't control who we love."

"You sure as hell could try."

"Then why'd they write all those songs?" she asks. *"Love and marriage . . ."* she sings, and then seems to think better of it. Even when she's singing alone, she sings the alto part as if we can hear the entire choir that's in her head. She holds one finger in the air and starts over. *"Falling in love again."* She gets that dreamy look. I hate her dreamy look. *"When I fall in love . . . Love makes the worrrllld go round . . .* No, wait! Wait! *Come on, bay-bee, light my fire . . ."*

"Mom. Don't . . ."

She's playing an air guitar. *"In the sunshine of your looooove . . ."* Her knees are bending, her hips are thrusting forward.

"Don't! Please! Mother!"

"She loves you, yeah, yeah, yeah . . ." She's snapping her fingers, thrilled because after years of trying, she thinks she's found the way to explain it all to me.

"Give it up, will you?"

"No. Love is the most important thing in the world." She stands up and her scissors fall to the floor with a *clink*. "If you only learn one thing from me before I die, I want you to learn that." She steps around the sewing machine and comes toward me like a barefoot pixie through the clearing we made in laundry baskets, paint cans, the panty hose rug, two-by-fours, hammers, putty sticks and spools of thread, rags soaking in turpentine—all her projects, her damned projects.

And I have a revelation so powerful we might as well be living right inside the Bible: my mother doesn't know how to give up. *That's what's wrong with her.* She's great at starting but she can't get to the finish line. It's all so simple. And I know how to fix her.

She stands there smiling across the ironing board at me, her hands on her narrow hips, little chin up high, and says, "What *about* all those love songs?" She thinks she's going to teach me about love and we'll all live together inside a song, drinking music, eating treble clefs, driving half-notes, dressed in scales.

I set the iron on its heel and walk around the ironing board toward her like Toto about to pull the curtain away from the Wizard. She'll hurt for a while but she'll be better off understanding the real world. "Mom," I say—kindly and in my softest voice. "Mom, those are just songs."

She keeps bouncing on the balls of her feet, rising up again and again, humming something sugary.

"Mom, they only write those songs to cheer people up. You feel good while you're listening, then *bam!* It's over! The song stays in the radio, you go back to your real life." She stops bouncing. "Look," I say, grateful that Dexedrine makes my mind so sharp that I can see everything in its true and logical order. "They're not cake recipes. They're love songs." She looks confused. "Okay, okay. Take, for example . . . Well, take loving Dad all these years. Where'd it get you?" I wave a hand around the living room. When I look back, she's staring at me. I push forward, brisk and icy-clear. Important things need saying. "And your boyfriend?"

My mind is a machine, totaling up her mistakes. Why did I wait so long? "Your boyfriend? Probably just using you. Give him up. Finish it!" She's getting weepy, so I wrap an arm around her shoulders. I'm on a roll. I'm fixing things. "Like having kids. You spend twenty years raising Randy and Mitzy and they move away and you get what. . . ? Five phone minutes a week? Collect calls? Hah! *I'm* never having kids." I pound myself on the chest. "Never. No kids. No husband. No fucking way. Not for this girl."

Mom pivots toward me. Shaking her head *no,* she pushes her face so close to mine it's as if she's trying to see inside my eyes. Tears are running down her cheeks.

I might have gone too far. I wrap my arms around her and pull her close. I'll have to hold her together until she gets through this. I rest my chin on top of her head. Her curly hair tickles my nose; it smells like Ivory Soap and cigarettes. Her narrow shoulders are trembling. She tightens her arms around my waist until I can feel her breasts nested underneath mine, her small hands pressed hard against my lower back. My name comes like a tortured sound from her throat, and I feel such a surprising tug in my own throat. I didn't expect it to hit her this hard. I hold her tighter.

She's warm as a cat against me, and crying now. "Shhhh, Mom. You'll be okay." I press my lips to the part in her hair. It's clear she's not through it yet. I rock her side to side, so warm in my arms. I slide my hand up to cup the back of her head. I tuck her face in against the base of my neck, and a flooding starts in my chest—a murky, burning flood that fills my lungs and expands my rib cage. It moves through my back, spreads up my neck, down my arms, until all I know is that I'll hold her like this forever if that's what she needs. I rock her. *"Dahhhh-dahh-dee . . ."*

1969

The Road out of Acorn Lake

*I*rene and I have been wasting our last year of high school looking for guys at a Minnewashka Valley dance club called the
Prison. Some local business wizard leased a big cement-floored
warehouse at the corner of 22W and I-94, painted bars on the
walls, dressed his waitresses in convict-striped miniskirts and
tank tops, fuck-me high heels and plastic handcuffs, and hooked
a revolving white strobe to the ceiling so he can play the *whoop-
whoop* escaped-prisoner alarm at the top of every hour. The man
knows how to extend a theme. Even way out here at the north-
west corner of Sioux County you can spot a smart one sometimes.
Natural smarts.

The bouncer shouldn't let us into the Prison since our fake
IDs fool no one, but he gets lax about carding whenever Irene
shows up, and I just ride through the door in her wake, imagin-
ing myself thin as a whisper again with alabaster thighs that

never chafe, upper arms without a dimple; and Irene has her head back, laughing over her shoulder, mesmerizing him with a span of Chiclet teeth and a mop of peroxided hair as we slip on into the smoky bar.

The only other place to find guys—new guys, not the ones we grew up with and out of in Acorn Lake—is the bowling-alley-slash-bar-cum-feedstore in Credit River, but that means twenty miles of washboard roads through wheat fields and hog farms and besides, the old coot who *is* the Credit River Police Department likes to stop underaged girls on that same lonely road after they leave Bud's Bowling and Brew. He's never touched anyone that I heard of; he just leans his head inside your window until there's no more room to back away. Then he shines his thick black flashlight up and down you real slow, going back and forth over the parts he likes, asking quiet questions like *Does your dad know you been over to Bud's again?* And then, *Maybe you girls would like me to show you the inside of my holding cell. Would you like that? As the chief of police it's my job to make sure juveniles don't drink and drive.* He always closes with *Remember, girls, I have been vested with the authority to arrest you.*

By the time you hear his boots crunching back to his black-and-white, you feel like you've been touched all over. Worse yet, you've been caught at it.

I'm not pretending we're virgins. I know I'm not pure enough to complain, and last fall after the homecoming parade Irene moved in with Benny Stillwater—Big Stick, she calls him now. You see, once you start, you give up the right to cry wolf. That's how it is in small towns. Everybody in the county knows Irene's living with that skinny Indian. People are still talking about how she hopped off the homecoming float, pulled out the bobby pins holding the queen's tiara to her peroxided hair, hiked her floor-length dress up to her waist and climbed up behind Benny on his Harley-Davidson—a chopped Seventy-four with a candy-apple-red gas tank and a twisted metal sissy bar that rose half a foot above her head when she leaned back, wrapped her extra-long legs around Benny's hips and tucked her bare feet into his jeans-covered crotch. Once you reach homecoming queen, there's no place else to go but bad.

The ninety thousand miles on the odometer and the rust climbing the door panels can't keep my '56 Chevy from starting, but I'm out of cash and low enough on oil to crack the block, so I'm here on the school bus and Irene will have to find another ride. I never touch my savings account.

It's 6:50 a.m. and I'm peeking through the hole I scraped in the iced-over bus window when Irene comes running out from Benny's shack behind the Paris-France Resort Cabins and flags us down. She dyed her waist-length hair Indian black and tied a blue bandanna across her forehead. All around her, fat snowflakes are drifting down, and as Wendell brakes and flips out the stop sign on the side of the bus, she stops in the middle of the road, holds her arms out to the side, tilts her head back, and spins in a circle, trying to catch snow on her tongue. As she runs up the bus steps she says, "Hi ho, new bus driver. Irene has moved to your neighborhood and any day of the week she could be waiting right here for you." Glorious. She passes him, then pauses in the aisle, turns back and says, "I could be," as if someone might try to make her go back home—maybe her father—but she's the ninth of eleven big-chested blue-eyed blond girls born to a failed hog farmer, and you can understand how they wouldn't notice one was missing.

We go to the Prison every Thursday, Friday and Saturday night, even though Irene's living with Benny. He loves her, but he's dealing hash and ludes, and eating up so much of his own inventory he can't tell if she's been gone for an hour or a day. She likes to say she loves him too, but you can see she's looking for more than what you'll find in Acorn Lake. She has a burning-up quality, an appetite so big I think of her with her mouth hinged open, arms moving like harvester blades, stuffing everything in life down into her throat—everything except food. Irene can smoke a cigarette in two long pulls and finish a beer with one tilt of her head, but it's her body that's ruining her life. Her body is so great that only brazen guys have the guts to approach her—the burglars and the drug dealers, the petty felons—guys who grab what they want. Nice guys figure they aren't worthy of a body like that. It's what makes them nice. It's what makes them dull. My own mother swears Mr. Right is out there, but my mother is always wrong about men. You won't spot a guy with enough criminal swagger to make your skin dance and enough farmer in him to let you sleep straight through the night. You have to pick one and ignore your ache for the other. At least that's what I decided; but I'm telling you about Irene.

Not ten minutes ago we walked into the Prison, and Irene's already locked eyes with a big pockmarked, square-faced, slit-eyed guy leaning against the wall, wearing a black leather trench coat and pushing thirty-five. Aretha Franklin's wailing through the scratchy low-end sound system, demanding some respect when Irene unzips her coat and lets her chest out. He jerks the toothpick from between his teeth, lets it drop to the floor, pushes down on his belt buckle with both hands, and lifts his shoulders—all in one move—rippling like a tomcat.

Suddenly they're facing each other, inches apart. He lifts one of her Indian-black braids from alongside her chest, holds it in the palm of his beefy hand as if he's weighing it, then gently places it behind her shoulder. It looks like he's been touching her hair for years.

The following Tuesday afternoon I'm sitting in advanced short-hand, taught by Mr. Jonas Bass, a neckless man with hair and skin the color of oatmeal. He's sitting on his desk, palming his beer belly, dictating a business vocabulary–building exercise to eight girls at a hundred words a minute, when Irene appears in the doorway like a surprise party. Poof! There she is, leaning against the doorjamb, one long leg crossed over the other, wearing knee-high white vinyl boots, a matching miniskirt and a white rabbit-fur jacket. She is new new new—from top to toe.

You're probably wondering why a girl with Irene's possibilities bothers showing up for school, but she's practical in her own way. She knows a high school diploma and solid office skills are the surest road out of Acorn Lake. The guidance counselor himself swore there will be high-paying jobs in the Twin Cities for girls like us once we add great typing skills to the off-the-chart verbal skills he saw on our ACT's. And Irene can hear a thing once and simply own it forever, so she never has to study.

We've spent most of our senior year with Mr. Bass. Aside from shorthand, he teaches typing and secretarial decorum. He says Irene has rare promise and gives her passing grades even though she's absent more often than not. One Saturday night before closing at Bud's Bowling and Brew, Mr. Bass bought Irene and me a drink and asked her if she'd like to go for a ride in his new blue Chevrolet Impala. That's what I mean about practical:

she maneuvered him like a bank shot, smiling the entire time. "Mr. Bass," she said, leaning close, "your wife is pregnant so often I speed-filed you under 'D' for dangerous." He collapsed in on himself, and we left him drooling into his beer while we speed-walked to the ladies' room, where we slid down the wall onto the dirty linoleum floor, laughing, crying, wondering when Bass would realize that she'd said no.

After shorthand class, Irene lets me try on her rabbit-fur jacket and the white vinyl boots in the girls' lavatory. The jacket is several sizes too small. "Nothing to worry about," she says. "Tall guys like big girls." My short boyfriend started ignoring me after my weight jumped fifteen pounds over the Christmas holiday. He never said a word when he ended it. Irene has to keep reminding me that he never said a word the entire three months we went together. In fact, no one has ever heard New Kid speak.

She lights two Kools and hands me one while she explains that the guy from the Prison is Willie, and he's in the women's clothing business—top of the line, furs and leathers mostly—and he's offered us a part-time job, and if there's oil in my car could I drive us back and forth the sixty miles into South Minneapolis. Irene hasn't saved a nickel for a car yet.

We skip out of school and head for Minneapolis. We'll try anything. We have boredom in common.

Our new after-school job is in the windowless basement of a house owned by Easter, an expensive-smelling Italian lady who shaves her eyebrows off and draws them back on with an auburn arch so high it looks like she's paying close attention to everything. You've never seen anyone so alert. She must be fifty, and she's lived all over the world. We've never met anyone like her.

She shows us how to use a metal stripper to remove labels from clothes—buttery soft leather coats, fur jackets with cool slithery silk linings, weightless cashmere sweaters in emerald green and topaz—and I know suddenly that I've never owned a single piece of good clothing.

We blow off school for the rest of the week and spend the days at Easter's. We fill a Tupperware salad bowl with labels and loose threads, and Easter empties it into the fireplace, staring down her long nose into the flames until everything is ashes. Saturday we work twelve hours, sleep in our clothes on her Hide-A-Bed, and get right back to work on Sunday. Small-town girls know how to work. It would be rude to ask how much we're making an hour, but we're betting on a lot more than the dollar ten we've been getting at the Acorn Lake Laundro-Matic. We know the clothes are stolen—Mr. Bass could figure that out—and any fool knows illegal jobs pay extra.

Sunday night, Easter hands me a brown wool sweater and a dyed-to-match skirt. "I have little else in size fourteen," she says. One eyebrow rises an inch and angles toward the front door. I leave Irene there, making a pile of size six leather jackets and skirts while Easter buzzes between duffel bags, picking out accessories—scarves, lapel pins, an alligator purse.

The following Friday, Irene is waiting for me after school in a silver Cadillac Eldorado, slouched down behind the wheel so none of the teachers will hassle her about skipping school. I slide into the passenger seat and sit up as tall as I can. It's Willie's car. He's decided Irene will live at Easter's. He'll see her whenever he drops off a batch of stolen clothes, and Easter will teach her everything she knows about the apparel business—not to mention giving her valuable tips on dressing and makeup.

Sitting inside Willie's Cadillac, with the engine idling softly and the heater blowing hot, Irene tells me all about her apprenticeship. It's St. Patrick's Day, and although it's only four o'clock, the air is that gunmetal gray that means the clouds are sagging, heavy with wet snow, and anybody with half a brain will grab some groceries and head for home because we're in for two, three days of road closings. But knowing you're in the path of a dangerous blizzard can spark you out of a coma. I slide down on the soft red leather seats so we can share our last joint on school property.

Irene laughs while she outlines a life without the pasty-faced, dead-eyed Acorn Lake boys and their skinny girlfriends, girls so naive they won't mind living their entire lives in this two-block town, like happily agreeing to stand on one of those moving walkways until you're eighty, riding on a straight gray line to death.

I take a deep hit off the joint and hold the smoke in.

Irene pounds the steering wheel with the heels of her hands and whoops twice, bleeding off some of her excitement.

I hear kids start their cars and drive away, but for once I'm not wondering if they're all going someplace Irene and I weren't invited. She lost her popularity when she moved in with Benny, and I'm not the kind who joins clubs. But even if you're bored with people, you want the chance to say no.

Snow starts floating down all around us, as if someone sliced the clouds with Easter's stripping tool. Millions of snowflakes are sliding back and forth as Irene and I run from Willie's warm Cadillac to my cold Chevy. It starts right up.

Irene wants me to drive her out to the Paris-France Resort Cabins so Benny won't see Willie's car. She says that way the realization that she's gone for good will come on him gradually, in bite-size pieces he can handle.

She convinced Willie to let her come back here one last time for her homecoming dress, her birth control pills and an armload of bangle bracelets she started collecting when she was thirteen. He let her out with orders to be back by nine o'clock and slipped two hundred-dollar bills inside a black suede purse along with the best counterfeit driver's license I've ever seen; it's a taste of her future. The license says she's twenty-two, but with her new false eyelashes and her arched-up auburn eyebrows, she looks old, and she's laughing too high, too much, like she raced from seventeen to thirty overnight, out of control in a sideways skid. She's already passed Acorn Lake, and there is no Plan B. I don't know if you can understand.

As she walks around the front of my car toward Benny's shack, passing through my headlights, the wind whips under her hair and lifts it straight up, two feet of coal-black hair standing on end, with glistening snow spiraling up around her body. She could be a sorceress. The wind heads off in another direction, her hair falls down around her face and after a second she comes back to my side of the car. I roll my window down a couple inches. She shouts over the noise of the storm, "If I'm not out in ten minutes, come inside and say we have to get going because you're worried about the roads." Her eyes are wide open, a layer of stark white snow trapped behind the curl in her black false eyelashes.

I turn off the headlights and sit listening to WDGY, worrying about bald tires, bad roads, and carbon monoxide fumes that are surely finding their way out through one of the cracks in my rusted tailpipe, snaking up through the apple-sized hole in the floor by my feet, draping themselves around my head like a toxic scarf, putting me to sleep by inches so I won't notice I'm dying alone. I flip on the windshield wipers; they plow the snow off to either side, but it's too dark to see. I wait ten minutes. I give it another five. Irene has never done anything on time, and suddenly I mind. Gray smoke starts puffing out of the round aluminum chimney near the edge of the shack's roof. I turn on my headlights, hoping she'll get the message; they shine directly on the plastic-covered window next to the crooked wooden door. I lean on the horn until Irene sticks her head out and gestures for me to come in.

I've never been inside Benny's. Irene always meets me at the road. The door slams and I'm in a smoky rectangular room with a plank floor and a curtained-off corner that must be the bathroom. Industrial-size green garbage bags have been stapled neatly up and down the two-by-fours that run from the floor to the ceiling; they make a *whoof*ing sound as the wind sucks them in and out. In the center of the room, Benny's lying on his side under a pile of dirty blankets on a mattress next to a wood-burning stove, his greasy black hair fanned out on the gray pillow. His eyes are half open and he's smoking sweet-smelling hash from the long tube of an elaborate hookah that must be a Vietnam memento; he came back a crazy-eyed sergeant after two tours. Irene says smoke and downers kept him sane. The brass water pipe with its coiled tubes is the only thing of value in the room—except Benny's chopper sitting on its kickstand next to a listing white hot plate littered with empty cans.

Irene shoves chunks of wood in through the stove's small steel door. "Benny," she says, "there's soup heating on the burner. Eat something. And you have to remember to keep putting wood in this fucking stove or you'll freeze to death." She kicks the stove door shut with her booted foot. I've never seen her angry before.

He puffs once on the pipe, smiles slyly and blinks, slowly. "Wood," he says.

Irene grabs her lumpy backpack. "I'm going out for a while."

As I back the car down the slippery one-lane driveway, Irene explains that she'll only stay with Easter for a few months—a year at most. She says she's learning ways to earn more in an hour than we've earned in three years of working part-time at the Laundro-Matic, more than a top-notch secretary earns in a year, that she plans to stash away lots of money—cash—enough to buy a car and maybe even make a down payment on a little house in the Twin Cities, and after she stops working for Easter and Willie she'll give me a piece of the house and we can work regular jobs and split the monthly bills—at least until we find husbands. It might take her a year to save up enough for all that, but she'll come out of it with so many good clothes that she won't need anything new for years afterward. That will save us money right there.

I drive through the storm, my nose to the windshield, straining to see the faint parallel tracks left by the last car, hoping they won't lead me off the road. Sometimes three, four, five cars will follow the same tracks into a ditch during a blizzard—like a wagon train of people who don't know that getting where you're going during a snowstorm means driving fast enough so you don't bog down and slow enough so you can stop if the edge comes racing up at your front wheels. It's mostly instinct.

I think about telling Irene she'd be better off going back to Benny, finishing her diploma, but I can still hear the garbage bags *whoof*ing on the two-by-fours. I concentrate on making it to the state highway where the plows work straight through storms to keep one lane open for emergency vehicles. Irene says she'll mail me cash every week and I should put it in a savings account in both our names over in the Minnewashka Valley State Bank where no one will ask questions. She's talking so loud. I wish she'd lower her voice so I can see the road better.

I flip on my high beams and catch a red flash off a stop sign, confirming that we're nearing the intersection of the county road and the state highway. I ease down the gas pedal to get the speed to make it up the rise and through the snowbank the plow would have left in our path if he'd gone by on the highway. We burst through it like the Starship *Enterprise* breaking through to another galaxy, with a thud, then a giving-way as snow flies up past the windshield like bits of the Milky Way. We fishtail making the left turn, but I steer into the skid and suddenly we're in the cleared lane.

And Irene has my shoulder, shrieking that I should come with her, trying to tell me Willie and Easter won't mind, saying she could convince them to take me too. She says it's the fastest way out of Acorn Lake. I tell her that when you're afraid of the new people you're meeting, it's sometimes a good sign that you're moving up in the world. If you're not scared, you're not doing something new. Finally she runs out of steam.

I stop in front of the driveway up to the high school. The snow is coming down more slowly.

Irene laughs, a short bark of a laugh. "Someday," she says, "you'll be a secretary to a really important man and Irene here will be a cocktail waitress in one of those fancy bars in downtown Minneapolis, someplace where all the men wear ties."

Before she gets out of the car, she gives me one of her hundred-dollar bills to open our account and says I should get my shorthand up to one hundred thirty-five words a minute, my typing to seventy with no errors.

I watch her race off through the snow, searching out the gullies the wind carves between the drifts, lifting one long leg after another, her black hair sailing out behind her like streamers.

Fully Bonded by the
State of Minnesota

*L*ying alone on a lounge chair on the deck of Willie's houseboat, I'm waiting to tell Irene I am *not* moving to California.
I have an entry-level secretarial position with an international
insurance corporation, a studio apartment in St. Paul, and a new
'69 Camaro financed back home through the Acorn Lake State
Bank at four and a half percent with four years of payments at
eighty-three dollars and thirty-one cents a month. I am set.

"Buy jewelry, buy leather coats, silver's good," Willie says to
Irene who's following him upstairs from the cabin. On the deck,
ignoring me completely, Willie turns and hooks a finger through
Irene's hoop earring, pulls her face up toward his until she's on
tiptoe, and kisses her until I want to fling myself overboard into
the cool clean water, wondering how any girl can kiss an ugly
man for so long. Willie's thirty-seven, six-foot-three, nose
smashed flat to a two-by-four face, pockmarks running up his
bull neck, over his face, under the coarse black hair he wears in a

crew cut even though it's 1969. He's dressed in skintight white swimming trunks and a fresh layer of sweat. On Monday Willie's Italian, Tuesday he's Irish, and Saturday night he's half Sioux, but every day of the week he's a full blooded liar.

Irene uses a laugh to pull away from him, making it sound like *Aren't we having fun?* and maybe she is having fun. These days whenever I talk about my white house, she shouts *F.O.B.!* That's Fear of Boredom. Today her hair's in pigtails—dyed-black fountains spraying off her head—a little-girl hairdo and big-girl cleavage, anything for fun. She's the only interesting person I know.

But I'm still not moving to California. I put away money from every paycheck—sometimes five bucks, sometimes twenty, but something every week—saving for a small white house, a paid-for house. One floor, one bedroom, one owner, no dust, no man who can't find his own goddamned sock drawer. That's my plan.

In the small parking lot across the road from the houseboat, Willie lifts two radial tires from the trunk of his silver Cadillac, rolls them through the dirt, then stands, stooped over, a finger on each tire, sneering at the tiny trunk of my orange Camaro. That car has a thousand-pound 302-cubic-inch V-8, a high-rise intake manifold and a Holley four-barrel carb—all of it under the hood, and a rear-end so short, so lightweight that if you tap the brakes on ice, she'll spin like a sweat sock with a toe full of rocks. You have to know how to drive a Camaro. I put towels on the backseat before Willie slides the tires in.

As I drive across the parking lot I tell Irene I'm not going to California with her. She's riding shotgun, and Willie's riding along in my rearview mirror, but shrinking as I pull away. I'm relieved he's not perched on the roof of my car like some evil flying monkey. He's a hard man to shake.

I punch the gas and squeal out onto the highway, loving the machine-gun spray of gravel until a horn screams and a dirt-brown Dodge Dart swerves around me. I should have looked first; I always look first because my policy has a fifty-dollar deductible and besides, once you bend a car's frame, it's over. Ask Dad, that car-killing, nasty son of a bitch who never once located his own socks. I pull out to pass the Dodge, doing eighty, eighty-five, ninety, the force of it melting me nicely into the quilted curve of my bucket seat, and suddenly Irene is dropping charge cards into my lap like flower petals, saying, "Use them while they're fresh. Willie said we need to use them while they're fresh."

I signal and pull back into the proper lane. "I am not using stolen charge cards."

She laughs.

A couple days later I'm at work early, grabbing overtime. I roll a sheet of bond paper and six sets of carbons behind the platen on my Selectric, longing for the manual typewriters Irene and I learned on in Mr. Bass's class. You could hit those keys hard and get a satisfying *dunk!* instead of the shallow *ticka-ticka* of electric keys that go only halfway down so you can spend the rest of your life typing and feel like you haven't done a goddamned thing. The old *dunk dunk dunk dunk BING!* made time go faster too; but Mom always says *Don't wish your life away.* More often though, she says *Do as I say, not as I do.*

The brown industrial carpet gives off a throat-clenching chemical smell under gray steel desks lined up, four rows of four, each with its own modesty panel. Mine's in the back. The girls up front get to type correspondence because they've been here over a decade; girls in the back type columns of numbers. I type a 2 instead of a 4, use the pink eraser stick on the original and all six carbons, leaving a trail of smudges. It's 7:05. I brush away eraser crumbs, roll the platen back around and type the correct number— a sixteenth of an inch *above* the line—rip the paper out, trash it, focus on inhaling and exhaling, trying to keep the tight fist in my chest from climbing up my neck and clamping down hard on my jaw as I put together another set of bond paper, carbon papers, tissue papers. The employee manual says secretaries are allowed one erasure per page.

I'm erasing my next big mistake when Irene calls. "Quit yet?"

"Fuck off."

"What you have to stick around here for I'll never know."

"Listen. I'm building a résumé and you need five years at each company or you'll look flighty on paper." I hear her take a deep hit off a cigarette. Someday she'll suck one inside out. Maybe it's a joint. I light another Kool, blow the smoke out my mouth and inhale it up my nose. "Nobody wants you unless somebody already has you, so you can't quit one job until you've got another one."

"Right. Lillian, put your cigarettes in your purse and split. No. Hold on a second. Why don't you just grab some supplies first; we'll be needing paper and envelopes. Scissors are good— and a stapler. Lil? Take one of those big staplers. Now tell me, do these people lock up their postage stamps?"

"Not having a job is proof that you can't find a job."

She laughs. "Hell, every town in America has a temp agency. Don't go sweating that one right now. We'll just drive west until we run out of money. Then we'll stop someplace and work until we're bored. Then we'll drive straight on to the next place." Irene says we'll take over a two-girl office in a western town. She'll be the receptionist, I'll type the letters and every night we'll have our pick of the cowboys because we'll be brand-new, new in every town from here to Hollywood. "Hah!" she says. "With our skills? Those folks won't know what hit."

It's true. I have an extensive vocabulary and excellent grammar, type seventy-five words a minute, and take shorthand at a hundred and twenty. Typing is like skipping rope: you have to stay alert and go brainless at the same time because if you really stop to think about what you're doing, your skills disappear. Humming helps. Amphetamines work better, and they keep my weight down, but I pay back two bad days for every good one.

Mom calls. It's eight a.m., and I'm straightening carbon sets again, leaving inky fingerprints everywhere like a moron at a major crime scene. "Honey?" she says like it's a question. "Honey?"

Am I a honey? I wonder. *Am I not a honey?* Mom is driving me crazy. *What the hell is a honey?* My life is stuck at eight a.m. and she's scraping a fingernail tip back and forth across the little holes in the mouthpiece of the phone. *Scritch. Scritch. Scritch.*

"Stop it," I shout. "Can't you just *talk* on the phone?"

She starts to cry. "Honey, do you have any whites?"

"No," I lie. I have six, but I'm saving them for Thursday and Friday so I can have two days of fun at work, two days thrilled by the way the ball leaps up to print black numbers in perfect columns on the clean white page, every page a masterpiece, two days of not having to wish I were the kind of girl who cared naturally. Every week I buy whites from Irene for my two-day reward, then spend Saturday and Sunday recovering for Monday. Two high days, two low days, three days of torture. When I gave them up for five months, there were no good days. But I will never be like my mother. She never learned how to plan her week, and she's not careful with her drugs.

"Honey," she says again. "Honey, I need you to baby-sit Davey on Friday night." Davey's twelve, and I don't like kids.

The other secretaries straggle in, carrying knitting bags stuffed with lunchtime projects: mostly macramé owls for hanging houseplants in front of café curtains above kitchen sinks all across the length of the Twin Cities, but the *front* row girls are studying decoupage together, already deep into Christmas trivets.

It leaves me breathless, and I have to concentrate on getting air, counting fifteen on the intake, fifteen on the out. "I can't talk now, Mom," I say, and light a cigarette off the end of the last one, never losing count.

At lunch I buy a map and sit in my Camaro, plotting a stolen yellow dry marker route to Los Angeles: nine hundred seventeen miles to Denver at seventy-five miles an hour—we'd be there in twelve and a half hours, or longer because I'd never let anyone drive my car, especially Irene. But the minute we hit Denver, time wouldn't matter because we'd already be someplace else.

It's 3:47. Everybody's trying to look like they're not packing up to leave, when Mom appears in the doorway wearing the one-piece skintight sleeveless powder-blue polyester jumpsuit she designed and sewed herself. She likes to tell people you can't buy jumpsuits like hers ready-made because so few women have the body for them and everyone knows the manufacturers cut for all those fat women. Her blond ponytail bounces when she moves her head—a little bird just looking for me. She discovers me, then waves at the entire typing pool—one at a time. "Hel-looooo," she says. "I'm Lillian's mother!" The decoupage girls raise eyebrows at each other, but the macramé girls wave back at Mom because they don't know how not to yet. She prances toward me like a majorette leading a marching band, shoulders back, legs spiking, clearly thrilled by the way her knees work, thrilled by every ratty little thing in life.

I escort my mother and her perfect body back out, holding her elbow in a death grip, through the lobby and out to her old beige Chevy Biscayne. I put her in the front, I get in back. Davey's in the passenger seat, drinking his bottle of Pepsi-Cola. "Hi," he says. That's all Davey ever says, except for *It'll be fine, Mom,* and *You look great, Mom*—in that voice that's supposed to keep people from tossing themselves off grain silos. If they want to jump, I say let them jump. Davey's always patting Mom's shoulder, and she's always telling him useless things like *If you're nice to other people, they'll be nice to you.* She's sure she'll get her reward in heaven.

"Why the hell aren't you in school?" I ask, leaning over the front seat between them. "Don't kids go to school anymore?"

He shrugs, then reaches up to move a loose strand of hair away from the lit end of Mom's cigarette. He looks closer, pinches off an inch of burned hair and wipes it away on his shirt, then turns to face the front of the car, waiting for me to leave.

"It's summer," Mom says. "School's out."

"Oh."

She hands me a small paper sack. "I brought you some *cook-ies!*" she says, wiggling her eyebrows so I get the message. "I managed to get your favorite kind from the pharmacist in Credit River. He likes me."

"Thanks." I take it. "But I'm still not sitting Friday night."

That night in Davidson's Department Store, Irene and I are spinning costume jewelry racks, trying on Monet, Trifari, Napier, frowning, shaking our heads, saying *It's just not you.* We like to try on things we can't have.

Irene's wearing a set of gold clamshell earrings bigger than cymbals. My mother says being tall is the kiss of death for girls and they'll never find husbands if they don't stay sitting down, keep their voices soft and never ever wear vertical stripes, long skirts or any jewelry above the waist. Irene turns her back to the saleslady and mouths, "These look real," then has the woman open the glass case for the matching pendant and a bracelet that's clamshells all hooked together on tiny hinges. I'm giggling, wobbly-kneed, remembering how we got caught stealing here a few years ago, and then Irene says, "We'll take these. One set in gold and one in silver."

As the saleslady rings them up, Irene whispers to me, "It's not like shoplifting. We have charge cards." Then, louder, "My friend here will pay for them," and then I'm forging the honest-looking, sticklike pen strokes of Gretchen L. Gunter, and ten minutes later we're on the road to Acorn Lake, jewelry under Irene's floor mat like no one would think to look there. She turns the radio up, and I turn it off. It's my car.

Fifty miles later as we cross into Sioux County, Irene puts on the gold jewelry, and in the dashboard glow she looks like a rich girl. She hooks the silver bracelet on my wrist because she knows

I'm mad. At an off-ramp Mobil station, I drop six charge cards into the ladies' toilet, kick the flusher, light two cigarettes and hand one to Irene. She grips it between her lips while she rearranges her hair in the scaly mirror, then shoulder-to-shoulder we smoke, staring down into the rusty toilet bowl, waiting for the cards to burp back up.

To find someone in Acorn Lake, you check Mel's first, even though he doesn't have a pool table. Hell, Mel hasn't got *any* tables—just a rectangular room with a bar in front and counters lining the walls where farmers drink side by side on stools, leaning toward the wall like it's the flank of a milk cow. There's no music, nobody says much. You can see how the top of a silo might look good.

Johnny Kale is in the corner. He grew up on a farm—feed corn mostly—but his dad sold it to somebody who planted rows of houses and now Johnny pumps gas at the Standard Oil for a buck an hour. Cash. Twelve hours a day, seven days a week, it keeps a wad of bills folded in his shirt pocket underneath his embroidered name. Johnny was born happy, so happy that he'll spend his whole damned happy happy life in Acorn Lake, grinning every time someone drives in over the fucking bell.

"Irene. Lillian. Hi." He's eighteen and bald with a full beard like cotton balls.

We lure him into the men's room. I lock the door. We model jewelry, tilting our heads, holding out our wrists. "It's hot," Irene says like she has to explain it even though we're wedged into Mel's stinking men's toilet at nine o'clock on a Monday night, whispering like Russian spies.

"Wow." Johnny touches the clamshell on Irene's neck with a long oil-stained finger, so excited he doesn't ask whether it's real, and you can't blame him; no one fences *costume* jewelry. He counts out a hundred in singles and fives on the wet sink while I wish I'd held back the silver bracelet. It sat on my wrist like a strip of cool water.

Irene boosts herself onto the sink then leans toward Johnny so fast it seems like her cleavage pulled her down. "We have a couple of radials left too. In Lillian's car."

"Twenty bucks," I say. He can sell them for fifty at the station.

Thursday morning Irene calls me at work.

"Keep the money," I say, having given it some thought. "And don't call me here. I'm fully bonded by the goddamned State of Minnesota."

She laughs. I love her laugh.

As I hang up, my phone rings again, but I slip my hand underneath and unplug my mother, not wanting to know whether she's up or down because all sixteen of us—four rows of four—are typing labels for a mass mailing by Samuel E. Silver, head insurance salesman. I'm chain-smoking, joyful, tossing coffee on top of speed, typewriter struggling to handle my lightning keystrokes because *I* am the better machine. Typing on speed is better than sex. I type through break, through lunch, straight on to seven o'clock and solitude, when Mr. Silver appears in his perfect navy blue suit, not an inch of fat showing anywhere, lots of wavy brown hair even though he must be forty years old. "Had enough yet?" he asks, and when I keep typing, he flips the light switch a couple times. "Go home, young lady," he says, but in a friendly voice. *"Go home."*

A few minutes later, I'm rapping off labels like it's this or death, when he appears at my elbow, briefcase in hand. "So you like to type?"

"Sure." I check the clock, wishing he'd disappear, planning to subtract his interruption from my latest time.

"Why?"

"Fun." If you're brief enough, people go away.

"You have fun typing?"

He's the head salesman, so I roll my chair back. "It's a game." I lift up my little clock. "Ten labels, two and a half minutes, sometimes three, depending on the address. Apartment numbers cost, but you need them."

"That's the game?"

"No." The guy must think I'm simple. "First, you get four rolls of labels to save three trips to the supply room. Set one behind the typewriter"—I point—"feed the end in here so the typed ones come out the top and flow back down into this box on the floor to save fiddling-around time between rolls."

He smiles.

"Most girls rip off a label, type it, rip off another, type it. You know . . ."

"I see."

"And I abbreviate the hell out of every word. I just shaved *thirty* seconds off of the last batch by leaving out punctuation. You don't need it."

"You were singing."

"Humming."

"Humming."

"So nothing distracts me."

"Like me," he says.

I shrug.

He shakes his head. "Honey, there are better games."

And suddenly I know I'm a fool for rattling on. I bite back a *fuck-you-I'm-gone.* "You don't distract me," I say as I put my cigarettes in my purse and head for the door.

Friday morning the Amundssen International Insurance Corporation benefits manual is on my chair with a bookmark. Under "Educational Reimbursement" it says in purple pen, *A better game!!!!!* I hate exclamation marks. My mother puts a string of them on checks right behind her big, loopy signature. She uses them on grocery lists.

> *PEPSI!!!!*
> *CIGARETTES!!!*
> *SNICKERS!!!!!!*
> *JACK DANIEL'S*
> *POP-TARTS!!!!!!!!*
> *RIPPLE CHIPS!!!*

That night in my apartment   a space so small I can pivot once and touch everything I have—words are going around in my head like a marble in a dryer: *What is a honey? Am I a honey? No one's honey. Honey honey honey honey.* But then the weekend crash starts, and suddenly hand-washing my panties in the kitchen sink doesn't seem worthwhile. As I dry my hands, I'm struck by the idea that someone interesting might be trying to reach me. You never know. And forty's not *that* old. The phone rings while I'm plugging it back in.

"Honey?" Mom says.

And I wonder why it is that the people you already love are the last ones you want to hear from.

There's the sharp *brngggg* of a gas pump bell. She's at the Acorn Lake Standard Station where Johnny Kale lets anybody use the phone. I can almost smell the gas and oil. "I need you to take Davey for the night," she says.

It'll serve me right if Johnny sells her the jewelry. She'll have to borrow the money from me and I'll have to pretend forever that she got a great deal on hot jewelry.

I remind myself that I pay the phone bill and the rent, I have a job, I own a Camaro. "I'm sorry, Mom," I say and hang up, and then I *am* sorry because any woman would deserve a night away from Dad, and what if she kills herself? People do it all the time. I head for the cupboard, having eaten close to nothing for two days, weight management a big benefit of my weekly speed system.

An hour later I'm finishing a box of graham crackers, watching my Arvin portable when someone bangs on my ground-level window. I turn off the lights, edge the curtain back, and look into my mother's upside-down face. She's standing in the window well, bent double with her nose against the glass. Rich people don't live in this neighborhood, but it is quiet and you can't have a forty-five-year-old Tinkerbell standing in your window well in a miniskirt and spike heels blackmailing you by shouting your name.

"*Shhhhhh,*" I hiss, my finger so tight against my lips it's like I'm trying to shush myself.

"Lillian," she shouts again.

I point toward the front door of the building, count to ten, press the buzzer, and by the time I've twisted open all the locks that failed to protect me, she's standing there, pushing Davey in toward me. "I'll pay you back someday," she says to me, then kisses me on the cheek and flees down the hallway, her tight red sweater tucked into her skirt, shiny belt around her tiny waist, loose blond curls bouncing. She stops, turns back toward me, strikes a Marilyn Monroe pose, wobbling on her high heels like she's playing dress-up. "Do as I say, not as I do."

"No kidding, Mom." I shut the door and press my back against it until I feel the solid click of the hardware and there's Davey standing against the wall, against my white wall like a small prisoner waiting to be shot. I stare at him, and in the middle of realizing that I've never looked at him closely before, it hits me that he's the same color from top to bottom as the dirt-brown Dodge Dart that almost killed me the one and only time I forgot to look both ways. I don't know a damned thing about kids except that Davey seems short for a twelve-year-old. His dirty bangs follow the curve of his eyebrows like he's cut himself windows. The sides of his dirty hair rest on the bulge of his baby-round cheeks. His fingertips peek out from the sleeves of a brown plaid shirt, its hem nearly reaching the tops of his over-sized, secondhand motorcycle boots, making it look like he might have been a bigger boy who'd shrunk in the wash—except that dirt is smeared across his upper lip like he's been wiping his nose with the back of his hand for days. He lifts his chin and looks into my eyes with eyes the same shape and color as mine, daring me, not angry, just holding his ground with his little chin up because he's standing on my carpet, in my apartment, on my Friday night, without an invitation. He nods once, businesslike, lips pressed tight. "Sorry about this," he says, and with a hard click I know that Davey will always be standing up against my wall.

Inside the paper bag he carries, there's a tablespoon stuck to a cough syrup bottle. He gives a phlegmy rattle to prove he's not faking. "It says take a tablespoon every four hours," he says. "So I'll need to know when it's nine twenty-five."

"It'll take you that long to get clean." I point toward my tiny but spotless bathroom.

While the water pipes creak and Davey's heels make hard rubbing noises against the floor of the shower, I unfold the Hide-A-Bed, shake open billowy clean sheets, and lift the soft cushions into the open space behind the head of the mattress. I plump every pillow, then step back to see what it looks like: not good enough, but when I turn on the light in the Budweiser wall clock I found next to a Dumpster behind a bar once, it comes alive with a gentle crackling, and my apartment glows warm and red. I'm inching the folding chair with the TV on it closer to the Hide-A-Bed when the phone rings.

"Where is she?" Dad asks. He's never called before.

"Who?"

"Your goddamned mother, that's who." There's a *clickety-click* as his highball glass hits the receiver and the ice cubes hit the glass, and I see his long upper lip rise up for a sip of Old Heaven Hill. "You're in cahoots together."

"Have another drink, Jack." I always call him Jack. "That'll bring her home." It's safer calling him Jack when you're sixty miles from Acorn Lake.

Davey walks out of the bathroom bare-legged, buttoning the shirt that looks like a tent dress, hair wet around the edges, dirt on his upper lip darker now from having been splashed. He's just a kid. God, he's just a kid.

I cover the mouthpiece. "Back in the shower."

"Is it Mom?"

"Use soap, Davey. And shampoo."

He stands, quietly, looking at me.

"Okay. It's no one. See?" I hang up the phone, then wonder why it took me so long.

Later, I find a *Little Rascals* rerun on TV, and Davey and I watch it, sitting together on the bed like it's a floating raft, surrounded by half a dozen paper plates covered with leftovers. We have a chocolate éclair, we have four slices of salami, two rubbery chunks of Kraft cheese and a short row of Oreo cookies, we have a heap of wet dill pickles canned in Wisconsin, and some ripple chips. We have a feast.

Davey eyes the éclair, looks at me, and waits.

I'm cross-legged, his foot in my lap as I cut his toenails, struggling with the one that's wrapped hard over the tip of his little toe like a tiny pale helmet. His feet are water-shriveled and warm; they smell like Ivory soap.

The red light flows from the wall clock, coloring the walls and the floor and the feast on the Hide-A-Bed, tinting us newborn pink. I nod toward the éclair. "Go ahead, Davey. It's just us." And I am set. Maybe I am set.

1970

The History of the Flood

I'm ankle-deep in water, wearing Dad's new rubber duck boots.
Mom's lying alone in their bed, blanket up to her ears. "Mom,"
I say, "there are nine reasons why you shouldn't commit suicide.
Number one: It'll mean you're a quitter. Number two: Dad will
have won." I lean down, lift the corner of the sheet out of the
muddy water and tuck it under the mattress. "Number three: You
have a great body and if you're dead it will rot. Number four:
Dead women can't dance. No cha-cha; no nothing. Number five:
Killing yourself is a mortal sin and you'll burn in hell." Mom says
with her nose all stuffed up, "Dat's for Catholics." "Five-B: It'll
be my fault for not stopping you, so I'll burn in hell. Numbers six
through nine: Randy, Mitzy, me and Davey." This part usually
gets a laugh. "We love you *so* much we'll leap into the grave right
on top of you. Mitzy will have to drive all the way from California
to the Acorn Lake Lutheran Cemetery, and Randy will have to get
here somehow from Minnewashka. God, poor Davey's only

twelve. And I won't get to live my perfectly planned-out life. I'll have to give up my apartment in St. Paul. My career will end at the starting line because I'll be down in your grave. I'll be the hood ornament on your casket. So if you look at it logically, it'll be quadruple homicide, not suicide."

Crying harder now, she rolls to the far side of the bed, and with her back to me, she curls into a fetal position tight as a fist.

All my old reasons have worn out, and I can't think of another one. Suddenly I want to lie down next to her, hugging my knees—just like her. I could drift off to sleep and forget that this place smells like a wet graveyard. Instead I stand here kicking the tile floor, watching the waves ripple off the toe of Dad's duck boot.

Spring flooding always starts around here with a sound like somebody's lunch being digested deep inside the walls, and you'll find Mom at two a.m., ear suctioned to the pine paneling like she's eavesdropping on her own house, or she'll say *hold that thought* and freeze, listening for rain. But this year Dad convinced her that the house wouldn't flood again—like he'll never take another drink, he'll only drink beer, only drink wine, never drink before dinner, never lie about his drinking, never drink and drive and the lower level of our house will never flood again—so Mom took everything down off the bricks.

But I don't live here anymore. I can pop in and leave again as soon as I please. I live just far enough away. This morning Davey called to say they were flooding, and sixty-two miles later I was going through the house clockwise, cupboard to closet, filling a grocery bag with every pill she owns. Dad has more guns than Colt and Winchester, but Mom would never use a gun; she's thinking *open* casket—halter top, satin pants, Revlon Talk-of-the-Town red lipstick, party smile, and a tear on her cheek, with the town women saying, *She tried so hard.*

"Wait!" I say. "Number ten: You could divorce the nasty son of a bitch, sell the house, use your half to rent an apartment on a dry hill for you and Davey, and when the money runs out, if you still want to kill yourself, I'll buy the drugs. And that's a promise."

Ding! Like a gate swung open.

An hour later Mom and I are leaning against opposite kitchen counters like always, smoking and talking, the room so narrow our toes nearly touch. I'm wearing the navy blue empire-waist, top-of-the-knee hopsack dress I put on for work this morning. I look like a fucking nun, but it's a uniform, like if you're a cop or a clown, and professional secretaries have to look like they mean business. I look pretty good right now anyway because my weight's okay.

Mom's in short shorts and a wrinkled polka-dot blouse, a housewife who won't wear a housedress. Her legs are walnut brown from the sunlamp she uses year-round. She claims she's walnut brown all over, but I don't want to know. She holds a piece of paper in front of her and reads out loud what we've written. She added the exclamation marks at the last minute.

DREAM HOUSE FOR SALE NOW!!!!!!!!
SEE THE WATER FROM EVERY ROOM!!!!!!!!

One-owner lakeshore home!!!! Cook while your kids swim!!! Dust while they skate!!! Vacuum while they slide!! 3BR, 1½ B, lg family rm only 4 steps down from main fl. Just 5 mi from downtown Acorn Lk! Owner will throw in: duck boat, duck blinds, fishing boat, umbrella tent, wooden dock, shovel, wheelbarrow, washer/dryer, auxiliary pump w/hoses. A little paint, some grass seed and you can have this dream. Best offer. Hurry.

We'll put the furniture on bricks, pump the place and sell it fast while Dad's on his fishing trip. It's lakeshore property, for god's sake—who wouldn't want to live here?

Mom will forge Dad's name on the documents. If he disputes it later, just like Perry Mason we'll swear into evidence samples of his signature going back to 1947 when Mom started signing it. He's that lazy. We make a pact: if forced to, we will hold hands and confess to the judge that Dad's been drunk for so long that he can't remember whether he signed his name or not. We've never told anyone he's an alcoholic.

Mom's reading the ad out loud for the third time when it hits me. "Mom, you could be a career girl too."

She stops reading.

"You can't be a housewife without a house to wife."

The inside edges of her bare feet flip up like heat vents. She wobbles on the outsides, thinking.

I say, "*Cosmo* tells housewives to list their experience." I grab Davey's homework off the rusted bread box. *Composition: Ten Reasons Why I Like Living on the Water.* He got an A. I flip it over to make a graph:

HOUSEWIFE	CAREER GIRL
Grocery shopping	Purchasing agent
Paying bills	Bookkeeper
Getting Dad to go to work	Personnel manager
Cooking	Chef

I fold the paper lengthwise. I crease it with my thumbnail. "Housewife's the bottom of the heap. No promotions, no paycheck. You can't quit without divorcing the boss and taking your direct reports along." I love business vocabulary. *Direct reports, tickler file, telex machine, stock-keeping unit.* I tear the chart in half, toss away *Housewife* and hand her *Career Girl.*

Ten feet away, Davey's in the living room on the davenport in his undershirt and corduroy pants, eating vitamins like peanuts, washing them down with Pepsi, and pretending he's not listening to us while he watches *Verne Gagne's Pro-Wrestling* on TV. He always swears it's real and I tell him it's not. How can he think people act like that?

Now he catches my eye. He's wearing his zombie look to convince the world he's calm, but he's wondering if Mom will be okay, so I lift my eyebrows and nod twice, looking even calmer than he does.

When I go closer to ask if he wants to overnight at my place, he shakes his head, just two tight little shakes. "Davey, she'll be fine."

Lips sealed tight as a tomb, he nods.

"Davey?"

"I know that," he says finally. "But my wrestling program isn't over."

"I'll be back first thing in the morning."

That night, sitting on my tangerine Naugahyde beanbag chair, I call Randy to see if he's in any shape to help. "Can you meet me at the lake tomorrow so we can pump the lower level?" He's still living in a farmhouse north of Minnewashka with seven other stoned Vietnam vets and eight shitty dogs. The place stinks like a barn and the basement leaks—like he never left the lake. I tell him we're selling the house when Dad's away fishing.

He says, "Wait . . ."

"We've only got fourteen days to open windows, run the fan, pump, mop, varnish over the water stains on the paneling, and Rust-Oleum the sinks, toilets and tub. Before everyone comes, I'll fill the rooms with lilacs to kill the smell." I have a list.

Randy says slowly, "Wait. I got it now," then sings every word to "When the Rain Comes." Then he says, "No. Wait. *This* is it." And after a long pause during which I hear rain hammering my windows and Randy puffing on the hookah he got in Saigon, he sings "Here Comes the Sun"—all of it, including high notes Tiny Tim couldn't touch. Then he says, "No, *this* is how it's suppose to be."

Randy helps me when he can.

I call Davey. I call him every night. "What's going on, kiddo?" He started spending weekends at my place last summer, and seems to like it even though I'm strict as hell. Every Friday I tape a tight schedule to my refrigerator, like this: Friday 6 p.m. pizza. 6:30 dishes. 7:00 *Hogan's Heroes*. 8:00 movie w/popcorn. 10:30 brush teeth, wash face, check finger & toenails.

"So," I say, letting the cord on my new white Princess wrap itself around my finger. "What's Mom doing?"

"Resting."

"Dad?"

"Came home and left again."

"What are you going to do?"

Paper crumples. "6 p.m. pizza. But no dishes."

"Smarty."

Most of the time he still hands out words like every one's a new chance to make a mistake. If I want to know what he's thinking, I ask him a long string of questions and watch his eyes. They're just like mine.

Saturday morning I pull into the driveway, hating the rain but loving the way it beads up on the Turtle Wax on my Camaro. I'm listening to the end of "Aquarius": *"Letttt the sun shine . . ."* when the WDGY Rock and Roll Weatherman interrupts to say the sun *will* in fact *shine in* by suppertime, and the rest of the week will be sunny and dry.

Davey's at the far corner of the house, wearing Randy's camouflage army vest, and Mom's barefoot in Dad's black slicker. On the small hill next door, Joan Hansen's in her kitchen window, looking down into our yard, watching little people in big clothes dig a deeper drainage ditch while she dries that same damned dish. Years ago I was standing right here when a roof rose over the farthest hill in the field—just a triangle at first, over a mile away, so I climbed the elm tree to watch until I could say for sure that it was a house.

Then Mom put the lawn chairs out and we spent the afternoon watching that house rise and disappear, rise and disappear, coming over the rolling hills, each hill smaller and closer. We didn't rush out to meet it—Mom, Randy, Mitzy, me and Davey—we just sat there in swimming suits in the summer heat with the rotating sprinkler set to hit our legs every ninety seconds while we drank Hawaiian Punch and watched that house come toward us.

Finally Don Hansen appeared, driving a truck over the last rise with the house following behind him, a two-story yellow stucco that had been pulled up by its roots. They planted it on the little hill so now Joan is looking down on us when Mom parks the tip of the shovel in the mud and runs with Davey and me through the rain and into our house. At least we built our own instead of dragging in a used one.

Inside, with water beading up on her cheeks like she's been Turtle-Waxed, Mom hands me three sheets of yellow tablet paper, typed on Grandpa's Remington manual. "I was up all night writing this to the IRS because they're sitting on our refund like they do every single year, but we need that money right now to fix up the house. Look, look, look. This'll *work*. It explains everything."

Dear Mr. Government Tax Computer,

You like to address your correspondence to Mr. Anderson. However, I (Mrs. Anderson) am writing to you in his stead because he works to support our 4 children—not to mention a labrador, 3 cats, a pet crow, 8 tame rabbits, and 2 foxes in a cage ((when they aren't hiding under our neighbor's quonset hut!!)). So-o-o I have to handle everything else. I would handle taxes anyway because I'm told I have a knack for numbers!

The year was, indeed, eventful! I had 3 MINOR fender-bender car accidents. Our eldest son, age 21 (home after serving his country as a Mortar-Man in the Viet Nam Conflict!!) had 2 accidents. I list all accidents under LOSSES, then I deduct them, as per Goverment instructions. Mr. Anderson rolled my VW Bug on an EXTREMELY icy corner in a BLINDING snowstorm. I suffered a broken baby-toe on each foot(Our MD says clumsiness is due to medication which I will explain after a breif history of the flood): Commencing with the notorious, Spring-of-1968-Thaw, the lower level of our residence became

flooded with 10 inches of standing water. Flooding
has continued intermittantly since '47 when Mr.
Anderson returned from WWII. We are immediately
adjacent to Acorn Lake—formerly marsh land, but Mr.
Anderson and I hauled in land-fill—inspite of which
it is VERY MUCH like living in the bottom of the
kitchen sink with the water running!!!!)

Stupidly believing it was over, we started
using our lower level, then _this_ year's Early Thaw
came, UNANNOUNCED! We see now that we should have
left the furniture on the bricks. It was, admit-
tedly, our mistake for letting our guard down.
Important things were lost, including rare photographs of the children, and receipts I had carefully saved for computation of taxes. Also, the
well-pump flooded out. However, that occurred _this_
year, and is, by the way, to be claimed as a LOSS
next year. Last Spring, the pump_motor_ went. In the
Summer of '67, the Evinrude, the toaster, the
ovendoor and our vacuum ceased to function. We got
4 NEW INCHES of standing water. The waterheater
failed, a wheel rolled off turning into the drive-
way(we thank God the baby won't be driving for
years to come!)and someone STOLE our Honda Mo-
Ped!!!!!

This explains our "Miscellaneous Losses".

Outside of these minor disturbances, we've
experienced minute problems, such as my nerves! And
my husband's!! It could drive a man to drink! This
brings me to the large drug and small doctor bills.
Our Doctor is a great friend who drops in to
prescribe exactly what we need but he never charges
a fee. Hence, low Doctor bills and large drug

usage. I suffer allergies and high-grade head-
aches, as well as poor teeth. (Seems I'd be better
off dead, but the children need me.) Also, Mr.
Anderson needs frequent tranquillizing, and <u>much</u>
Excedrin, all of which shows up on pharmacy bills
scotch-taped to pages 9-36 of The Return.

But, all in all, it looks as if we will
survive in spite of oursleves! Things couldn't get
more confusing, in fact, we feel much more smiley
since having made the unanimous decision to put our
JINXED House on the buyers' market and move toward
the Cities where life can't be like this! God is
watching out for the Andersons! In the meantime,
I'm doing the best I can. But you could help me by
remitting our refund ASAP!! ($332.89.)

End of story!!!

Thanking you,
I remain,

Mrs. Jack (Marion) Anderson

Mom is bouncing on her toes and showing me every one of
her perfect little white teeth. She smacks her palms together and
says, "Bing, bing, bing. That oughta get 'em in gear. My daddy
was a writer—okay, *proofreader,* but only because we were in a big
depression and now I'm going to be a writer."

"You need a real job."

"Bet you didn't know your mother could write like that."

I didn't. So I bite my tongue, not mentioning yellow tablet
paper, improper salutation, excessive use of the exclamation
mark—I hate that—or that Mitzy sold the moped before she

left—like it was hers to sell—or that you don't get to claim your kids if they leave home. I don't want to upset her, but I can't help saying every single date is wrong, and nine and a quarter inches was the highest the water got. "If you don't believe me," I say, "check Randy's high-water mark: June 3, 1968 9¼." He carved it in the paneling at the end of every flood season.

I'm about to mention a few more things when her face goes blank the way it does when you pop her balloon. I should have saved my list for later. Now one eye looks huge, like she's had a concussion. Maybe she had a fall. I pull her closer. But it's only black mascara smudged below one eye and not a scribble of makeup on the other, making her look off balance. I kiss her forehead as if nothing's wrong. "I couldn't have said it better." That's a lie, but the IRS won't read past the first paragraph anyway.

By two o'clock the drainage ditch is deep enough. We're going to grab some lunch, then mop the floors. Mom and I are in the family room watching Davey push-broom the last inch of water toward the pump when the motor coughs, then cuts out, and the silence wakes Dad right up. He moans, "Oh, Jesus" from the bedroom, then appears wearing boxer shorts, a hangover and his duck boots. "What the *hell* is going on here?" Seeing people work bewilders him.

The three of us are standing shoulder to shoulder. I elbow Davey like Randy used to elbow me, Davey does it back, I elbow Mom, she elbows me, and because we keep our moves small and our faces straight, Dad just thinks we're fidgety and not too smart.

Dad always says water seeps through walls because that expensive extra-thick block-sealing tar doesn't grow on trees. Then he says *For your information, neither do those pricey six-inch underground drainpipes, the good clay ones.* He says the roof leaks because asphalt shingles don't grow on trees, and wind whistles through the knots in the pine paneling because fiberglass insulation doesn't grow on trees. Every last thing that can break in a house is broken in ours because money for those overpriced-sneaky-thieving repairmen, the ones Mom would call at the drop of a hat if Dad didn't watch her like a hawk, well, that money doesn't grow on trees either.

Then he looks out the picture window with his hands in his pockets like he's checking the branches of the oak trees, hoping something will change. But as Randy says, you won't find get-up-and-go growing on those trees either.

Now Dad's at the front door, fully dressed. As he buttons his raincoat, he shakes his head and looks up past us like he's talking to the elk head on the wall. "For Chrissake, the gas you're burning in that pump is so rich you're going to asphyxiate someone." He waves his hand in front of his nose as if we've poisoned him, then heads out the door, probably going to Mel's Bar to sit with the farmers facing the walls, milking their beers. Dad likes to go there wearing a white shirt and tie.

The door slams, and I'm still rolling my eyes when Davey turns to me and says what he always says, "Dad's doing the best he can."

I say, "For God's sake, no. No, he isn't, Davey."

That night at my apartment, Davey's brushing his teeth, and I'm scouring the kitchen sink when the phone rings, and the operator asks, "Will you accept a collect . . ." and Mitzy's shouting, "You can't sell the *house,* Mom said you're selling the house, Mom says you're selling—"

"Whoa, Mitzy. Pull up."

She sells prescription drugs and oatmeal-marijuana cookies from studio apartment 2B in Venice, California—*a block from the boardwalk,* she always says. Three dollars a pill, cookies free if you hang around to hear about pontoon floats, rabbit-trapping, ice skating for miles in the moonlight, breathing from just an air pocket under a flipped-over fishing boat, and two pet foxes in a cage (when they aren't hiding under the neighbors' Quonset hut!!!!!!!!!!!!!!!). We're like *Little House on the Damned Prairie* in the brains of two dozen hippies and a girl from Paducah who sleeps in a Dipsy-Dumpster *immediately adjacent* to the boardwalk.

Mitzy's shouting, "Who said you could sell the house, who the hell said you could sell it? Who—"

"Mitzy."

"It's not yours to sell. It is not yours. You're not the queen of everything. You can't—"

"Well, I can't just *fucking well leave them* living out there either."

But she's off again, telling me how she tells them about it. "—orange butterflies on purple lilacs, pussy willows, snow angels—"

"Mitzy."

Her voice ripples, "It was so beautiful. Wasn't it beautiful, Lil?"

"Yes. It was."

I hang up, and see Davey watching me, toothbrush against his front teeth, elbow out to the side. Mom shouldn't have waited so long to have him.

Sunday morning the sun is out, and by ten, Davey and I are showered and shampooed. We've brushed our teeth, used the carpet sweeper, done the dishes, and washed a load of white cottons in hot-hot water and Hilex bleach. We've done it exactly that way for months. "Always remember, *this* is how people do Sunday," I tell him and he nods. Then I wait because he's set his lips together in a certain way—carefully, perfectly, which means he's thinking. Finally he says, "Then they go to a matinee movie."

At the Mobil station, we buy a *St. Paul Pioneer Press* from the box. "Pick it: war or comedy," I say. "Then we'll go to the lake." We're going to work every night this week.

Two hours later, in the parking lot after the war movie, Davey stops, and I stop midstep like we're laced together. "*And* the comedy," he says.

So we go.

On Wednesday at the St. Paul office of the Amundssen International Insurance Corporation, I'm at my desk in the back row, wondering why they call this a bullpen, then fill it with girls. I'm chain-smoking Kools and typing actuarial tables—pages of numbers telling people how long they'll have to work and when they'll die. This one gives Mom another thirty years to live—assuming she'll want to. They give Dad twenty-five, but he'll hang around as long as she does, making sure she's pouring coffee from the correct side—right to the end. I get a little thrill when I picture her walking out. I'm never getting married. Housewives need rules. Number one: If at any time more than forty percent of your house is flooded, and if at the same time rain is running down more than one of your walls, then you may pour your husband's coffee from either side. Number two: If at any time the rubber boots next to your bed float away in the night, you do not have to cook breakfast. Number three: If your husband fools around, you can too, but only once.

I'm concentrating hard when hail hits the building like buckshot, flushing fifteen secretaries from metal nests, papers flying like feathers as girls flitter toward the window. I find my hands pressed hard against my chest. Exhaling, I set them on the keyboard, then jump again when rain starts as if it were thrown from a bucket.

It's been raining since Davey and I came out of the comedy on Sunday afternoon, only easing up every few hours like a runner slowing to take a breath. We've pumped water and mopped wet walls at the lake for three nights, but we're losing ground. Last night the drainage ditch caved in.

I type faster, bounce my thighs, and try to think about actuarial tables, but I know the rain is sneaking through the shingles and seeping through the walls. I want to open my mouth like a window and scream until my hair stands out straight.

It's just the NoDoz. And the numbers. And the rain. I should be out at the lake.

I rest my forehead on the pebble-grained plastic top of my steel-gray Selectric. It's warm and vibrating from the power running through it. As I sit back up, my plate-size hoop earring loops the end of the platen and I screech in surprise—like bad brakes on a big truck—and the entire clump of girls looks this way, backlit by the window, fifteen as wide as thirty should be. I was fat once. I'm still a fat girl. I'm just not fat right now. I'll bet they all hired on thin, but eight hours of typing makes a jelly donut look like a diamond ring.

Judy Darter's wondering why I screeched. She's walking toward me, her thirty-six-inch strand of pearls bouncing off the ledge of her chest. She wears expensive suits. I want expensive suits. I swallow my gum and take the cigarette from my lips because I've memorized page ninety-five of *Your Secretarial Guidebook:*

> You may never chew gum. You may, however, smoke at your desk because this will waste less of your employer's time than running to the ladies' room. At no time should you type with a cigarette hanging from your lips.

Ms. Darter's been with Amundssen International Insurance for twenty-six years—which means if Mom decides to live out the thirty promised by this table, she's still got time to be a Judy Darter. So do I. I check the table: forty-seven years until I retire. They always give you bad news in numbers. I do the math in my head. This can't be right: in 2017 I'll still be a Judy Darter, a twenty-first-century Darter. She's walking toward me faster now, elbows out like she's struggling hard through breast-high water. Probably walks that way from twenty-six years of pacing the bullpen forty hours a week, watching sixteen slow-moving fat girls type numbers that fog the truth about death and retirement.

Two hundred and thirty-four wordless pages of wall-to-wall numbers are sitting on my lap when it hits me that all I like about business is business vocabulary. That's it. Only the words. "I'm just sick," I tell Ms. Darter as she rows up to my desk. I pick up my purse and stand. "And my mother's flooding," I add like an idiot.

Five minutes later, I'm doing sixty-five in the rain, heading for the lake. I've blown almost a year of my life typing numbers, but tomorrow I'll get up early, skip work, and make a bullet-pointed list of career options. The more bullet points, the more options.

The Rock and Roll Weatherman apologizes for the rain and promises clear skies by nightfall.

I'm doing seventy. I took my Camaro up to a hundred and twenty-eight once. On dry pavement. That would be suicide in the rain, and I'm not the suicidal sort. I hate waste. I kick the car up to seventy-five. A cop I dated last winter said tires plane in the rain at fifty-five—like fifty-four is safe—but I learned to drive on a frozen lake in a Volkswagen Bug. I'd hit the brakes and steer into the spin. Now it's second nature. I love to drive. All you need is a radio in a rust-free car and twenty-nine cents for a gallon of gas.

When I pull into the driveway the auxiliary pump is in the yard, straddling the pipe leading down to the cesspool, and jumping like a tin wind-up monkey. The cesspool must be filled to the rim with runoff from the melting snowpack and weeks of hard rain. Humming the nasal sound of "When the Rain Comes" just as loud and fast as I can, I leap the six green garden hoses Mom strung together years ago to stretch from the cesspool pipe across the yard and the dirt road and into the field. This is the law: Even if the farmer's field lies fallow because the government pays him not to farm, you cannot pump your cesspool there. So we try to do it after midnight with a mound of throw rugs muffling the motor. The Hansens are asleep by ten. *Cessspool.* A word so ugly Mom wouldn't have said it to the IRS if it doubled her refund. Now Joan Hansen watches me as I run through the rain. When I look up she turns away, and I think I'd like it better if she weren't so kind.

Inside the house it's a cave—not a light on anywhere and the drapes half drawn. It's warm and moist, with the hard, steady sound of the pump coming through the walls, and the rotten-egg smell of the cesspool backing up into the shower. If I were a better person, I'd pack up Mom and Davey. I'd let them live with me in my bright white studio apartment until she finds a job or we sell the house. I wish I could, but I'm not that nice. And they'll be out of here soon. As I wait for my eyes to downshift into the gloom, I decide there's no such thing as smell; you're just tasting tiny pieces of whatever you breathe up into your nose, but it's one of those things people don't discuss. Like a cesspool. I stop breathing. I cover my nose and back outside to stand beneath the eaves, bent over with my hands on my thighs, staring at my businesslike navy blue pumps and the hem of my perfect career dress. I'm breathing hard, but with all this rain so close to the lake, the air is mostly water.

I straighten up and focus on the tip of the umbrella clothesline, exhaling, inhaling, folding in blinders until I'm staring down a tunnel at a black pinpoint. You can handle a pinpoint. It's the shortest plan. Like this: Mom and Davey and I will have dinner at the Acorn Lake Drive-In, sitting in my lemon-scented Camaro. We'll eat hot crunchy french fries drowning in ketchup, fish burgers swimming in tartar sauce. We love tartar sauce. Then we'll plan our next step.

Back inside, as I lean to turn on a lamp, I hear the gentle slap of sandals running down the stairs. I spin and in the shaft of second-story light, white strappy sandals appear, then walnut-brown calves flexed by spike heels, then brown knees, tight white miniskirt, red belt, white blouse cut too low, red fingernails, matching lips, curly blond hair.

"Got a job interview?" I ask and turn on the light.

She stands on the wide bottom step, clutching her clutch purse, her mouth a startled red O, answers racing through her mind. I know her cluttered mind. Now she's blinking fast—I've seen it clear her brain like someone kicking a coma. Finally she lifts her chin and says, "Sort of."

My watch says five-forty.

"Sort of a meeting," she says, and her lips close like a little drawstring purse.

"With Biff?" In the two years since I caught them, I've never said his name. An ugly name, like *sniff. Biff.* I knew it wasn't over. "A *meeting* with Biff?"

She steps off the bottom stair, trying to make her neck as long as Audrey Hepburn's. She has the *My Fair Lady* album and she can sing every word of every song. She believes it really happened—Mr. 'iggins and the flower girl and the special way it rains in Spain.

Suddenly Davey's behind her—at first just stocking feet and tan corduroys coming down the stairs.

"Mom," I say. "Hold it. Wait a sec." And I nod toward him.

She looks over her shoulder, then back at me. "Mr. Brookes is *a very good friend of mine* who's been teaching me how to place a residential property on the real estate market."

Davey sits on a middle stair in his sleeveless undershirt, props his elbows on his knees, sets his chin on his fists and watches us.

Mom says to me, "It's a lot more complicated than *you* realized. Selling a house isn't all that easy." She's spinning things around on me. I know her mind. I see it through her bright-green eyes just before she glances down at my shoes. Once, fast.

I look down at her sandals, then straight up into her eyes. "So what did your good friend Biff say?" His name's been stacking up somewhere every time we thought it at each other. Now we're overflowing with *Biff.*

"Biff is going to give me an appraisal."

"He's going to tell us what our house is worth?"

Davey stands up. He wants to live here forever with Mom and Dad. He's never said it, but I know.

"Hey," I say. "Kiddo. Hang on a second. Davey? Why don't you come home with me tonight?" But he disappears up the stairs. Maybe he thinks if he's in the house it can't be sold. You can't sell a house with a boy in it. You can't even leave your old davenport.

"Biff has a college degree." Mom takes two steps forward. "In economics." Another giant step for mankind.

"Has he *seen* this place?" My arm sweeps out and knocks over the lamp. I scramble to stand it up, struggling because the base is too narrow. We should have tossed it years ago, but it was a wedding gift, and lamps don't grow on trees.

"Biff hasn't seen the inside of this house for twenty-four months." She can't even say two years; it's *twenty-four months*— like a seventh-grader. First time we held hands: June 3rd. First time we kissed: June 3rd. First time he saw my all-over walnut-brown tan: June 3rd.

I'm holding the lamp steady. "Mom, I'm not talking about the last time he was here."

"Biff's driving all the way over here tonight just to appraise it—free of charge, as a favor to me. He can do a walk-through in five minutes flat." She snaps her fingers in case I don't understand speed. "Afterward we're going out to dinner to discuss it. At someplace nice." Then she adds, "Jack won't get home before midnight."

"I just meant I didn't think you'd want Biff to see you living like this—"

Her head swivels to the side as if I threw something at her. Then she looks at the floor.

"It's just that you don't know how bad this is. You can't even see it anymore. Look. Look around you." She won't look up. "Do you want Biff to see you living like this?"

She starts to cry, folding in on herself like a candle melting.

"Mom, I'm sorry." I can't reach her, and the lamp will fall if I let it go.

She bites her lip, trying to stop crying.

"I'm sorry. I know the house isn't your fault." I'm trying to think of something to say that will fix things. Her lower lip slides out into a pout. She looks so helpless.

"Wait a second," I say. "*You* think Biff's going to take one look at all this and carry you off on his white horse. Don't you? Don't you? You're not worried about fixing up this place and selling it. You've got your own plan. Don't you? You *want* him to see all this."

Her head comes up fast, and for a flash, I see the naughty six-year-old hoping this can be our little secret. She knows I love a plan.

"Are you out of your mind?" The lamp rolls over like a bowling pin. I set it back up; it's the only light in the place.

She covers her mouth with her hands and starts to cry, changing so fast I don't dare look away. But this time I know it's real because it makes her face ugly and launches tears down the grooves between her fingers. Her hands slide down until they're folded like bird's wings over her neck. "Biff loves me. And he would *never ever* let me live like this . . . When he sees . . ."

"Like I would?"

With the back of her hand to her runny nose, she hiccups. "The minute he sees . . ."

"Wake up, will you? Biff Brookes is the oldest bachelor in the county. Will you wake up? He's never ever going to *rescue* you. You have to save yourself. We had a plan. First," I say, jabbing a finger into the air. "First: You find a job while we fix up the house. Second: We sell the house. Third: You and Davey get your own place in the city. You have to save yourself."

I've got three fingers pointed toward the ceiling like some idiot Boy Scout making a pledge. My other hand is stretched out steadying the lamp. I'm straining hard, trying to think of something that'll make her understand, when I realize she's no longer crying. She's dead still, not making a sound. I've never seen my mother awake and so still.

She walks toward me slowly. She's wearing spike heels, but her steps are so solid she might be a woman in a tweed suit and flat shoes. As she gets closer, coming into the light from the lamp, it looks as if her makeup and her tan have disappeared; her face is one pale color—lips, nose, cheeks, forehead. "Lillian." Her voice is low and calm. "Honey, please. Listen. No one is going to buy this house. Period. I have one hundred and seventy-three dollars. I have a twelve-year-old son."

"You can get a job."

"Like yours?"

I can't even make myself nod.

"I went to an employment agency yesterday. They tested me. I type twenty-eight words a minute with twelve errors. And I don't take steno." She's ticking things off on her fingers. "I don't know anything about business vocabulary, and waitresses don't make enough money to rent an apartment and feed a son—not in the Twin Cities, not even in Acorn Lake."

"But Dad will have to pay you something."

"Wait." She stops me with her eyes. "When I leave Jack, there won't be anyone here to get him out the door to work. If Jack doesn't sell hardware, they won't pay him, and then he won't be able to pay alimony or child support. And when he can't make the mortgage payments, the bank will take this house. I've thought this out. I can't leave here on my own." With her hands on her hips, she looks down at the floor, shaking her head. "Did you think I was stupid?"

"What—" My voice is shrill as a tin whistle. I say, "What do you *want*? What the hell am I supposed to do? Just tell me!"

She lifts her head. "You're supposed to leave."

Backing out of the driveway in heavy rain, driving a Camaro like a coffin. Have to remind myself to drive. On the highway I hug the wheel, my speedometer at fifty, but my insides paralyzed as if the pistons are hammering and the brake is on, my mind a loop, saying to Mitzy, *Well, I can't just fucking well leave them at the lake, can I? Well, I can't just fucking well leave them at the lake, can I?*

I'm paralyzed—except for this gentle rocking against the wheel. I crank up the radio and drive for miles with the bass pounding in my chest like a borrowed heart. Hendrix, Joplin, Black Sabbath, the Stones.

The old cloverleaf is my halfway mark. I loop all four sections just to feel the heartbreaking pull before I shoot out onto the eastbound freeway. Sixty, sixty-five, seventy. This is how it's supposed to be—fast, and so free there's no way my tires could be touching ground. Seventy-five, eighty, and way out over the legal limit, I keep checking my mirrors, but no matter how fast I go, the house is still there, as hooked to my bumper as the Hansens' used yellow stucco. At a sharp curve, it disappears—but it's back in an instant. And when the light hits my rear window at just the right slant, it will seem to be gone. Or over a long string of hills, the house will rise and disappear, rise and disappear, and rise again.

ACKNOWLEDGMENTS

I would like to thank the other Lippka kids —Jeff, John, Mary Margaret and Dan—for their loving encouragement; Sam Stoloff, for his gentle patience; and Jordan Pavlin, for her insightful editing and for knowing which parts are funny. There are many others whose friendship and advice have been essential, among them Lou Mathews, Lauren Cobb, Rachel Resnick, Paul Arenson, Bill Audeh, Mark Danziger, Phil Rowe, Shelly Lowenkopf, Leonard Tourney, Jennifer Shull, Grace Rachow, Mashey Bernstein, James Coffey, Valerie Hobbs, Judith Kirscht, Dean Pananides and Susan Chiavelli.

A NOTE ABOUT THE AUTHOR

Jean Harfenist grew up in Minnesota. She is a graduate
of New York University. Her stories have appeared in
*Quarterly West, Nimrod International Journal, Wisconsin
Review, Prism International, Crazyhorse, Sonora Review,
Hayden's Ferry Review, The Cream City Review* and else-
where. She lives in Santa Barbara, California, with her
husband.

A NOTE ON THE TYPE

The text of this book was set in Garamond No. 3. It is not a true copy of any of the designs of Claude Garamond (ca. 1480–1561), but an adaptation of his types, which set the European standard for two centuries. It probably owes as much to the designs of Jean Jannon, a Protestant printer working in Sedan in the early seventeenth century, who had worked with Garamond's romans earlier, in Paris, but who was denied their use because of Catholic censorship. Jannon's matrices came into the possession of the Imprimerie nationale, where they were thought to be by Garamond himself, and were so described when the Imprimerie revived the type in 1900. This particular version is based on an adaptation by Morris Fuller Benton.

Composed by Stratford Publishing Services,
Brattleboro, Vermont

Printed and bound by R. R. Donnelley & Sons,
Harrisonburg, Virginia

Designed by Iris Weinstein